UNTIL
FURTHER
NOTICE

by
G. Weiler Hogan

Mother Pete Press

This book is a work of fiction.

The book also refers to these compositions:
I Feel Pretty (Bernstein/Sondheim)
The Girl From Ipanema (Abbott/Jobim)
It Had To Be You (Jones/Kahn)
The Ballad of Gilligan's Isle (Schwartz/Wyle) a.k.a. the theme
song from *Gilligan's Island*

The Midnight Ride of Paul Revere is the work of Henry
Wadsworth Longfellow (1807 - 1882)

Library of Congress Control number: 2010936530
ISBN: 978-0-615-39971-3

Mother Pete Press
Guerneville, CA 95446
motherpetepress@gmail.com

UNTIL
FURTHER
NOTICE

Prologue: Where Boys Marry Boys

WHERE BOYS MARRY BOYS

May 17th, 2008

Nancy Lou has gone off to California. I tried to talk her out of it, but she wouldn't listen to me, or to her mom either. I don't know how she is going to survive in a place like that, where they just passed a law that says boys can marry boys and vice versa, and where practically everybody is a Democrat.

I've known Nancy Lou since we got acquainted in Miss Clara Brown's English class in tenth grade. I liked her right away and she liked me well enough, I guess. We started to spend a lot of time together, shopping at the Super Wal-Mart whenever we had some spare cash and doing our nails and talking about boys. I figured we'd still be hanging out long after we graduated from high school, but I just didn't realize how much of an itch Nancy Lou had to get out of our little town and see the world. Me, I'm strictly an Oklahoma girl, and don't have any wish to go traipsing from one MacDonald's to another so I can say I've seen the sights. I can see all the sights I want to right here in Landon. But Nancy's different. Five minutes after we threw our hats in the air at graduation she told me, "Emma, I've been doing a lot of googling, and I've decided not to take that job at Mr. Hopkins' shoe store. I'm going to drive to California instead. There's a little town in the north part, near San Francisco, called Riverville. It sounds cool. There are only 91 women to every 133 men, according to the last census, so it should be pretty easy to meet guys."

"But Nancy Lou," I protested. "You have a perfectly good boyfriend right here in Landon, namely Henry Thomas Hampton the third. And he wants to marry you."

"Oh PLEASE! Henry is just not a California boy. On the other hand, my dear Emma, I've always been quite sure that I was meant to be a California girl."

I knew then Nancy just didn't have any idea what towns with okay sounding names like Riverville can have in store for people like her who have never been farther away from home than Wal-Mart. But like I said, Nancy wouldn't listen to me, or to anybody else. She was headed west, and that was that.

THAT'S HOW EASY IT WAS

"My name is Nancy Lou Walker, and I just got here from Landon, Oklahoma. I'm a real good waitress, in case you need one. Back home I worked at Big Al's Ribs after school, and all the customers wanted to sit on my side of the restaurant, I guess because I'm a friendly kind of person, and also, I always made sure they didn't have to wait forever for their orders to get there. So if you happen to have an opening for a personally qualified hard worker I'm available."

That's what I told the cashier at the Three Bars restaurant in downtown Riverville.

"Well, Miss Walker, you just might be in luck," he said, flashing me a big smile. "Tourist season officially begins this weekend, and we're going to need extra help." He was blond and tan and was wearing a dress shirt with starched shorts and flip-flops. "Let me see if I can find Joe. He's the boss, and he's the one you need to talk to. My name's Peter Jensen, by the way." He smiled at me again, and went off to find Joe.

In a couple of minutes they were back. I stated my personal qualities all over again, and the boss said he'd give me a try starting with brunch on Sunday. That's how easy it was to find a job in Riverville. Now I just needed to find somewhere to live, hopefully not too far from the restaurant so I can walk to work and save on gas.

I asked my new boss if he knew about any apartments for rent, but he didn't. He said his wife was visiting her mother in San Francisco and I could stay at his place if I wanted to, but I knew better than to do that. Gosh, did he think I was that dumb? I told him no thank you.

I bought a newspaper at the Safeway store across from the restaurant, and looked at the ads. But I didn't see any apartments for rent in my pitiful price range. Maybe, I thought, if I walk around town for a while, I'll see a for rent sign or something. And guess what. That's just what happened. Only five minutes away from the middle of town I saw a sign that said, 'City Beach, two blocks,' and right under it, taped to the same post, was a little piece of cardboard.

'MEMORANDUM,' it said.

'To all prospective tenants: John De Angelo, owner of Smoke Hill Cottages, wishes to announce that he has a studio apartment available beginning May 15th. We are located one block straight ahead on the south side of the street.'

I decided to get my car, which was still parked across from the restaurant, and drive over. It was the twenty-second already. I hoped the apartment was still available.

The place wasn't hard to find, and it looked okay, really kind of homey would be the way I'd describe it, several little cottages in a row on both sides of a wide driveway, with front porches and a patch of well-kept grass in front of each one. Not too fancy for people like me with a lack of money.

I found the office and knocked on the door. A tallish man maybe fifty years old, with blue eyes and salt and pepper hair cut real short, answered.

"Are you Mr. De Angelo, the owner?" I asked him.

"Nope. I'm the manager," he replied. "Can I help you?"

I told him I was interested in renting the studio

apartment, and that I already had a job at the Three Bars restaurant, and did not do drugs or anything else, including pets. I also told him I thought I had enough money for the security deposit and the first month's rent, if it wasn't too much. That was all I had to do. He showed me the studio apartment, which is real cute, even if it is pretty tiny, and I said I'd take it. That's how easy it was to find a place to live in Riverville.

The manager signed me up for a year's lease, gave me the keys to the apartment, and said, "Welcome to Smoke Hill Cottages. I'm Richard Stamp, general manager and, some folks say, general pain in the ass." We both laughed. He seems nice, and he has awesome blue eyes, even if he is old enough to be my father.

Mr. Stamp says it's okay to park in the handicap parking for a few minutes while I bring my stuff in from the car. I think I'll stay here tonight. The electricity is turned on, and I can sleep in my sleeping bag on the floor. Or maybe I'll blow up the air mattress Mom made me bring. I'll call Mom on my cell phone tomorrow and tell her I'm okay. I think I'll call Emma, too. Or maybe I'll just e-mail her. Because she'll probably already be at work by the time I get up.

6

I wonder if any single guys live here, or if it's all couples except for me. Mr. Stamp says there's a pool. I wonder if there's a hot tub, too. I hope there is.

BOBBY

When I woke up the next morning the sun was streaming in through the open Venetian blinds. I really am in California, I thought, and smiled, nestling a little deeper into my sleeping bag. It felt like about nine o'clock.

I knew I should call Mom. It was already eleven in Landon, and today was the day she had lunch out with her friends.

I got up and went into the bathroom. That's when I noticed all those little brown bugs running around on the floor. Oh yuck, I thought, I'm going to have to tell the manager about this because I don't want to step on them with my bare feet. But first I have to call Mom.

I dialed the number and told her I was okay and already had a job and an apartment right by the river, and would she please send my things from Oklahoma. She said she would, but then suddenly she was all full of worries about me. Maybe I was just pretending to be okay. Maybe somebody kidnapped me and was making me call and say I was okay. Maybe there were cockroaches in my new apartment. Mom is like that. She gets these ideas, and the thing is, what she worries about never happens, but she sure gets close sometimes. Like, I know those bugs in the bathroom are not cockroaches, they look more like some kind of outdoor bugs to me.

I told Mom not to worry, that I really was okay, and I loved her and missed her, and how glad I was to be getting the rest of my stuff from Oklahoma as soon as possible.

"Nancy, Honey, have you met any nice boys yet?"

"MOM! I just got here! I have to hang up now. My phone is going dead."

"Nancy, wait..."

"Bye, Mom," I said.

I pulled on my jeans and a t-shirt. Then I went to the front door and opened it. That's when I saw the piece of paper taped to the outside. It looked like it might be a bill. But I didn't think I owed anybody any money. I pulled it off the door and unfolded the paper. It wasn't a bill; it was a note from Mr. Stamp.

'MEMORANDUM,' it said.

'To the new tenant in apartment K: Please be aware that it is not appropriate to park in the handicap space overnight unless you have an official DMV placard issued by the state of California. I'm sure this was just a one-time oversight on your part. Again, welcome to the Cottages.'

It was signed, 'Richard Stamp, General Manager.'

I could feel myself turning red. How could I have forgotten to move the car? I put on my sandals, grabbed my car keys, and flew out the door.

After I located my assigned parking space and moved my car there, I decided to check out the pool. I was thinking about the little bugs in the bathroom. Maybe I could catch one and put it in a jar or something and ask the manager if it's a pinching or biting kind of bug that might crawl into my bed, once my bed gets here.

The gate to the pool was open, and a little boy about nine or ten years old, with red hair and lots of freckles, carrot top we would call him back home, was playing in the pool. When he saw me he grinned.

"Hey," I said. "Where's your mother? The sign says, 'Children and pets must be accompanied by their parents and owners in the pool area.'"

"She's in bed," he said. "She has a hangover." He got out of the pool, and walked over to me.

"I don't know you. Are you new?" he asked.

"Yes," I said. "I just moved in to apartment K. My name's Nancy. What's yours?"

"I'm a MacKenzie," he said proudly. "Us MacKenzies is nuthin but trouble. My daddy says we's the most trouble this shitty town has ever seen."

"Yes, well, do you have a first name?"

"Robert Ronald is it," he replied. "But everybody just calls me Bobby. Do you have a dog?"

"No, I don't have a dog." He looked disappointed. "But I do have some bugs I want to show Mr. Stamp. You can help me catch them, if you want to."

He grinned.

So that's how I first met Robert Ronald MacKenzie. He and I walked over to my apartment, put a couple of the bugs in a paper cup, took them to the office, and showed them to the manager.

"Where did these insects come from?" he asked.

"From my bathroom, right by the tub," I answered, thinking he wanted an exact location. But Mr. Stamp wasn't looking at me; he was looking at Bobby.

12

"I didn't do it! I didn't do nuthin," Bobby wailed. "Why do I have to get blamed for everything that happens around this stinking place?"

"Because you're usually the one who is causing the stinking problem," said Mr. Stamp. "I'll have the insects out of there right away, Miss Walker," he assured me.

And sure enough, he did get rid of every single bug. Now my entire apartment smells like that awful stuff people put on their hair when they have cooties. Of course, I never, myself, ever had cooties, but I knew somebody in third grade who got them from her cousin. I'm not going to tell Mom about this, and I don't think I'll tell Emma, either. She doesn't have to know everything, even if she is my best friend.

I wonder if Bobby's mother said it was okay for him to go swimming all by himself. And I wonder if Bobby really did put the bugs in my apartment, like Mr. Stamp seems to think. Why would he do that, anyway?

ROGER

This morning there was another note taped to my door. Now what did I do? I wondered as I unfolded the paper. But it wasn't just to me.

MEMORANDUM

To: All Tenants:
The water will be shut off tomorrow, Wednesday, June 4th, from nine a.m. to three p.m. This is necessary because some people have been experiencing temperature surges while in the shower, and we are trying to determine why this is happening. Bathroom facilities will only flush once after the water is shut off, so try not to use them during the designated time period.

Thank you for your cooperation,
Richard Stamp,
General Manager

Mr. Stamp's note made me laugh. That's a long time not to pee or anything, I thought. I bet we're going to have a lot of flushing happening after the water gets turned back on.

I should tell Mr. Stamp that I know somebody who is knowledgeable about plumbing, in case he needs help solving his water problem. The guy's name is Roger, and I just met him last week. He works at Home Depot in the plumbing fixtures department. I can hardly wait to tell Emma about him: black, curly hair, and blue eyes, and almost six feet tall. Besides big arms that make you want to get crunched inside a Roger bear hug. I met him when I was working at the restaurant and he came in with a couple of buddies for the Wednesday night special, which is all-you-can-eat-ribs. Of course the Three Bars ribs aren't anything much, not like Big Al's in Landon, but people here don't know the difference so they think they're pretty good.

Anyhow, last Wednesday Peter Jensen and me were both working the dinner shift, me waiting tables and him at the cash register. As it turns out, Peter lives at the Cottages, right across the street from me, and drives for the lady in apartment E to make extra money. Why she can't drive herself around I don't know, and I was just about to ask Peter about it when Roger and his buddies came through the front door.

As soon as I saw him, I knew I was going to go out with him. I've been in Riverville for almost two weeks, and he's the best thing I've seen yet. Don't get me wrong. There are just as many cute guys walking around in this town as anywhere else, more even, but the trouble is, most of them like boys better than girls. I didn't get it at first, but I figured it out after it just got too obvious.

Like I said, as soon as Roger came in I knew we were going to go out together. When I took his order I could see he was looking at me the way guys who want to take you out do and I made sure to let him know I liked it. But then nothing happened. After Roger and his friends finished their dinner, they stood up to leave and at first I thought that was going to be that. Oh well, probably he decided I have too many freckles, I was thinking. But Roger didn't go out the door with his friends. Instead, he caught my eye and motioned for me to come over to where he was by the cash register.

"I didn't get your name," he said.

"It's Nancy."

"Well, Nancy, that new movie, the one about Los Angeles being attacked by giant worms from outer space,

17

is playing at the Cinema Six. I've been wanting to see it. Could you go with me tomorrow night?"

Well, of course I knew I could. I don't work on Thursdays, but even if I did, I would have just called in sick.

But what I said was, "Well, I don't know. You haven't even told me your name."

"Roger," he said. "Roger Wills."

"Well, Roger, I'll have to check my calendar. Why don't you call me later tonight?"

He grinned, and I gave him my phone number. I didn't ask him for his because I didn't want him to think I had nothing better to do with my time than to put guys' phone numbers in my cell phone.

Of course Peter heard every word.

"Not bad," he said. "I wouldn't mind going out with that boy myself."

I laughed. "Well, you can't have him, Peter. He's mine."

I wanted to call Emma and tell her about Roger when I got off work, but it was already almost midnight in Oklahoma. So instead of calling Emma, I congratulated myself with two glasses of red wine, which

18

is supposed to be good for you, according to the heart association and other knowledgeable people, and tried on my gaucho pants to see if they still fit. Then I went to bed.

Well, we saw the movie last Thursday. Giant worms are not really my thing, but Roger loved the part where the worms spread slimy stuff on the streets and cars were slipping and sliding all over the place. We held hands and later I let him kiss me goodnight. I hope he asks me out again. Or maybe I'll ask him out, but next time I get to pick the movie.

THE CRITTER PATH

MEMORANDUM
To: All Tenants
From: Richard
Date: June 10th, 2008

Adam Jefferson, in apartment C has suggested we have a yard sale next Saturday to celebrate the beginning of summer. Please stop by the office or leave a message on my phone with a yes or no vote and whether you can provide tables or anything else for this event.

Also, Betty Carmichael, in apartment I, reports hearing 'scuffling and scratching' noises in her bedroom closet at night. She is currently sleeping on her living room couch while we attempt to find the source of these noises. It has been suggested that the scuffling might be coming from underneath Mrs. Carmichael's closet, not from inside it. Sometimes small mammals and even larger ones such as opossums can decide to make their homes under people's apartments. Please let us know if you hear scuffling and/or scratching so that we can promptly investigate.

Also, we are in need of someone who is smaller than my assistant, Jimmy, and not afraid of spiders, to crawl under apartment I and any other apartments where noises are being heard. Any volunteers?

Richard Stamp,
General Manager

I don't see why we have to vote about the yard sale. I say just let the people who want one have one, and the rest of us don't have to go. Adam wants to have a barbecue afterwards. Maybe I will go to that.

I like Adam. He's from Tennessee, and he has long strawberry blonde hair which he sometimes wears in a ponytail, but mostly doesn't. He's a couple of inches taller than me, about five feet ten, and has what I guess you would call a medium build, only maybe a little bit skinnier. I met him in the parking lot a few days ago, and we talked about the yard sale. So I already knew about that, but I told Adam I don't have anything to sell, being so newly moved in.

"Well, shoot, Miss Nancy Lou, that's purely understandable," he said.

Just then, little Mrs. Carmichael, who is at least seventy years old, got out of her car and walked, or I should say wobbled over to us. She was so loaded down with shopping bags from Safeway she could hardly walk, and Adam and me offered to help her with them.

"Thank you, sweethearts," she said in a shaky voice. "I really am all tuckered out. Didn't sleep again last night."

22

"Why aren't you sleeping, Ma'am?" asked Adam.

"Because of those animals in my closet," she said. "They're so noisy."

I was thinking, well, she's an old woman and she's imagining things. But Adam didn't see it that way.

"Miss Betty," he said, "we had best take a look see. No reason you should have to put up with the likes of critters in your closet."

"Well, Adam, that's very kind of you. But they seem to go away in the daytime."

She looked at me. "You'll probably think I'm just imagining things, Nancy. Is that your name?"

"Yes, Ma'am."

We brought Mrs. Carmichael's groceries in and put them on her kitchen counter. Then Adam politely asked permission to open her closet door and have a look. Of course there was nothing in there except her clothes and her shoes and a couple of suitcases.

"Here's what we'll do, Ma'am," Adam said. "We'll make a pathway between the closet and your back door for the critters to follow. You got any cardboard boxes?"

"I do," I said, and went to get them. When I got back to Mrs. C's apartment Adam was busy constructing barriers on each side of the critter path. He was using the suitcases, some couch pillows, a couple of dining table leaves and stacks of magazines. I added the cardboard boxes.

"There you go, Ma'am," Adam said. "You're all set fer tonight. What you have to do when you hear 'em is open the back door, then open the closet door and jump out of the way real quick, and those pesky animals will stop their scufflin' and scratchin' and will likely head out of here so fast you won't even see 'em."

Mrs. C was smiling. "Thank you, dear."

I was smiling, too. And I was liking Adam more and more. I'm pretty sure he's gay, though. Oh well. But I wonder if gay guys are always just gay or if sometimes they like girls.

When I got home, I checked my e-mail and saw that I had a message from Emma.

'I guess now that you are having such a fun time in California you don't have five minutes to send an e-mail to Oklahoma and tell me what you are doing,' it

24

said. 'For your information, what I, who used to be your best friend (remember me?), am doing is being bored.'

'Emma,' I wrote back, 'I have been pretty busy with my job and everything. I did try to call you. You should answer your phone more often. But what I've been doing is seeing Roger. He is so cute, Emma. I'm going to send you a picture of him so you can see what he looks like. We're going bowling tonight. Isn't that cool? That's what my mom used to do when she was a teenager, go bowling with her boyfriend. You are still my best friend, Emma. Don't be silly.'

Some weird stuff has been happening around here lately, not just Mrs. Carmichael's critters. This morning when I opened my front door I found three little sticks of spearmint gum in their wrappers on my welcome mat. I don't like people leaving stuff around in my personal space; it gives me the creeps.

THE WOMAN IN APARTMENT B

Yesterday, I met the woman who lives in apartment B, Evonna Courtland. I've been wondering about her, because she always seems to be dressed up. People in Riverville pretty much wear jeans all the time, or at least most of the time. Maybe she has a job she has to get dressed up for. Or maybe she just likes how she looks in a dress. She does have the kind of shape guys really notice.

Anyhow, yesterday I was looking for Richard because I wanted to tell him my closet door is off its track, when I saw Evonna on the other side of the Cottages driveway, waving at me, her bangle bracelets sparkling in the sun. I crossed over and said hi.

"You're Nancy, aren't you," she said, smiling. She had a Jackie O. kind of voice and sunglasses to match. "I've been hoping to meet you. Welcome to our little neighborhood, such as it is. I was just thinking about going downtown for a cup of tea. Would you like to join me?"

"A cup of tea?" I asked. Because everybody I've met so far in Riverville is into coffee, not tea.

"Well, yes. Herbal tea. It seems to soothe my nerves. But the coffee shop does serve coffee, too, if you would prefer that. Isn't that wild?" She laughed, and then laughed some more. I didn't understand what was so funny, but I laughed too, to be polite, and accepted her invitation.

The coffee shop is only a couple of blocks from the Cottages, but you have to pass by the five and dime and the drugstore and the bookstore to get there. So that's when I found out Evonna doesn't pass by any place that is selling stuff without buying something. By the time we got to the coffee shop she was carrying a bag with wrapping paper and ribbon from the five and dime, another bag with several bottles of nail polish from the drugstore, and still another bag with a romance novel from the bookstore.

The coffee shop was crowded, so we decided to take our drinks outside to a little table on the sidewalk.

"I like to be outside," Evonna said. "These dinky little places give me claustrophobia."

"So, how long have you lived at the Cottages?" I asked her.

"Oh, I've only been in Riverville since February," she said. "And at the Cottages since March."

"Where are you from?" I asked.

"From?" she repeated. She looked startled. "Well, I lived in Washington for awhile, the state, not D.C., but I really don't like to talk about it," she said. "I had some bad experiences there. The man I worked for was not a nice man, and I had to quit my job. And then people said…."

She began to move the bangle bracelets on her arm, turning them around and around.

"Do you need anything for your coffee?" she asked me.

I shook my head.

"Then I'll just get a bit more sugar for my tea."

When she came back with the sugar she was frowning. "I'm afraid I have to leave you now," she said. "So sorry, I seem to have a bit of a headache. But let's do this again. It's been ever so much fun. Really."

And then she left.

THE BEST SEATS IN TOWN

MEMORANDUM

To: All Tenants
From: Richard Stamp
Date: Friday, June 27th, 2008
RE: The Fourth of July

Greetings,

The Fourth of July will soon be upon us, the biggest day of the year at the Cottages, this year especially, because City Beach is going to be closed and we will have the best seats in town for watching the fireworks. Security will be very important. Please tell your INVITED guests that they will have to identify who they are coming to see and which apartment you live in before we will let them through the front gate.

Also: No potato chips in the pool area.

Also: Absolutely no dogs may be anywhere on the property at any time. Please be considerate of our cats.

Sincerely,
Richard Stamp,
General Manager

Another memo! It sounds like we live in an institution or something, with people having to say who they know before they can get in. And why do we have all these silly rules about potato chips and dogs and other stuff?

Yesterday, Adam told me that Mrs. Carmichael's critters have moved over to apartment H, according to Bobby. How does Bobby know, I wonder? The people in apartment H moved out last weekend, so there's not even anybody there to hear things in the closet.

I guess Mrs. C is glad her critters have gone away, but now she has a fly problem. Last Thursday was my day off. By nine a.m. it was already hot, so I decided to go swimming. That early in the day, I would probably have the whole pool to myself, and nobody would see how I look in my Macy's swimsuit since I gained six more pounds. My grandma always said we should be happy with what God gave us in the way of a body, but I sure don't like how much body I have. I weigh one hundred and thirty eight pounds now. That's with nothing on and after I pee and with my hair completely dry. I feel like a blimp.

When I opened the pool gate I saw that Richard and Jimmy Jones, the kid who helps him take care of the yard, were doing something to the deck, replacing some of the boards, it looked like.

"I thought it was your day off," I said to Richard.

He nodded. "Yep. But Mr. D wants to make sure nobody falls through the deck while they're watching the fireworks and then sues us. So we're working overtime."

Richard's phone rang. He pulled it out of his pocket and answered. "Stamp here," he said. Then, "Mrs. Carmichael, this is the third time you've called me today. This is not an assisted living facility. When you rent an apartment at the Cottages you are expected to open your own pickle jars and deal with the ordinary problems of daily living, such as flies."

I could hear Mrs. Carmichael's voice on the other end. Then Richard started talking again.

"Mrs. Carmichael, Betty, we removed the screen door to your deck at your request so that you could, as you put it, 'enjoy the great outdoors without a barrier.' When you leave the deck door open and there is no screen between you and the great outdoors you can expect an occasional fly to come in. Why don't you just swat it?"

Mrs. Carmichael went on talking, and I could see Richard was getting impatient. He was almost yelling now.

"Look, Betty, that's what flies do. They fly around and around and make buzzing noises. That is not alarming or erratic behavior for a fly. But okay, I'll send Jimmy over."

"Why doesn't she just swat it?" asked Jimmy.

"She says she wouldn't want to smash the life out of a defenseless little thing like that."

"So she wants me to smash the life out of it."

"Right."

Jimmy headed for Mrs. Carmichael's apartment, and Richard went back to work on the deck. I draped my towel over a lounge chair and dived into the pool. I wanted to ask Richard about the parking rules for overnight guests because I think Roger is going to ask if he can spend the night tonight. But I decided this wasn't the right time. Richard was probably still feeling pissed about Mrs. C's fly problem.

I swam a couple of laps. Poor Mrs. C, I was

thinking. I bet she hasn't had anybody but herself in her bed for twenty years at least. It must be hard to be old and all alone. I should stop by and say hi sometime. I could tell her I don't like how flies act either. And I could ask her if she has a family somewhere and if she likes living here at the Cottages.

When I got out of the pool I saw that my neighbor, Evonna, was talking to Richard. Then I noticed something else. Richard wasn't acting like his usual 'I am the General Manager' self. Instead, he was being all smiley and flirty. And Evonna was giggling. I could see this was still not the right time to ask Richard about overnight parking. I left the pool area and closed the gate behind me. I don't think they even noticed I was gone.

It sounds like the Fourth of July will be a lot of fun. Adam told me they're going to shoot the fireworks off from our very own beach, so we really will have the best seats in town, like Richard says. I wonder if I should have a party. Pamela Parker, the lady Peter drives for in apartment E, said she's having a dinner party for her book club friends 'appropriately themed to the occasion.'

I wonder what that's supposed to mean. Red, white and blue decorations, and little flags all over the place, I guess.

THE SECRET

Evonna invited me over to her place for dinner last night. I thought maybe Richard would be there because they seemed so cozy with each other when I saw them by the pool the other day, but he wasn't. It was just the two of us, Evonna and me. Her apartment was crammed full of stuff, not just furniture, but all kinds of stuff: posters all over the walls, knick-knacks everywhere, piles of newspapers and magazines on the floor, and red, white, and blue crepe paper streamers draped across the ceiling.

I looked at Evonna. "Are you getting ready for the Fourth of July?" I asked.

She laughed. "Does look that way, doesn't it, or it could be I have a special fondness for red, white and blue." She winked at me, then opened a bottle of wine, a Fetzer Cabernet, and poured us each a glass.

"Sit down, Nancy," she said. Then added, "I suppose you think I'm a clutter junkie."

"Oh no," I lied.

"Actually, I guess I am. It makes me feel, I don't know, safe I guess, to have a lot of things around me. I hope you like fish. We're having red snapper for dinner. Fortunately, the ants aren't attracted to fish."

"You have ants?" I asked.

"No, I don't. But Betty Carmichael does, and she lives just across the street from me, as I'm sure you know, no distance at all for a determined ant to cover. I hate ants. But I don't like to squish them. I think it's bad Karma to kill things."

She ran a well-manicured hand through her long blond hair and leaned toward me. She was wearing a lot of mascara and bright red lipstick. Without the sunglasses she looked more like Dolly Parton than Jackie O, I thought, but with smaller boobs, of course.

She leaned closer. "You do like fish, don't you Nancy?"

"Yummy," I said, lying again. I was beginning to wish I hadn't come.

She laughed.

"Nancy, I want to tell you a secret, but you have to swear you won't tell anybody else. Okay?"

"Okay." I was thinking about how my grandma told me once not to be a fool for secrets because sometimes people wish later they didn't tell you and don't like you for knowing, but I can't help it. I just love to hear people's secrets.

"Are you sure you won't tell anybody, Nancy?"

"Yes," I said.

"Really, really sure?"

I nodded.

"Well then, here it is: Richard Stamp, our General Manager, is going to ask me to marry him, and I think I'm going to say yes. And Nancy, I haven't mentioned it to Richard yet, but I'd like to be married right here, at the Cottages. Would you be my maid of honor?"

I gulped. "Your maid of honor? We hardly know each other."

Evonna smiled at me. "Well, we will just have to get better acquainted, won't we? Our dinner is ready. Let me make sure the windows are latched so the raccoons don't try to get in. Then we can sit down. Raccoons do adore fish, you know." She was whispering now. "Though I wouldn't want them to hear me say that."

We sat down and I choked down a couple of bites of blah-tasting snapper while Evonna went on and on about her wedding plans. I washed down another couple of bites with a second glass of cabernet.

"Are the raccoons watching us, do you think?" I asked, hoping to change the subject.

She looked at me, eyes wide. "Are there raccoons around here?" she asked. "I imagine we should tell Richard about it if there are."

I stood up. "I have to go now, Evonna. Thanks for dinner."

"But we haven't had dessert yet," she protested.

"That's okay," I said and left.

After I got home I called Emma. She sounded sleepy. I keep forgetting how much later it is in Oklahoma.

"Emma," I said. "I think one of my neighbors is crazy."

"Scary crazy?" she asked.

"Yes."

"Maybe you should call the police, if he's scaring you."

40

"No, Emma, it's not a he. It's a she. And she's not scaring me exactly."

"She's just making you feel weirded out?"

"Yes."

"Well, why don't you call Roger?"

So I called Roger. And told him about having dinner with Evonna and how first she talked about raccoons trying to get into her apartment and then acted like she didn't even know there are raccoons around here. I didn't tell him her secret, though. I wouldn't do that.

"She sounds spooky," Roger said. "Do you want me to come over?"

I did want him to come over. "If you're not too busy."

DAY-AM!

Thank goodness the Fourth of July is over with.
Who would've thought somebody would set off a whole
string of firecrackers on Mr. D's front porch, of course
breaking a window, on our national birthday? But
somebody did. Richard thinks it was Bobby, and maybe
it was, but I wonder how he could get those kinds of
firecrackers that are made in China and you can probably
buy in San Francisco but not in Riverville. And he's just
a little boy. He doesn't have any money to buy things
from the illegal people on the street. But who else would
do such a thing? As it turned out, though, that wasn't
the only excitement we had that night, before the
fireworks show even started, I mean.

About eight o'clock, just before dark, Roger and
me went to Adam's apartment to watch the fireworks
from his back deck, since Mister D had so many people
over to watch the show, there was not enough room on
the pool deck for us regular residents. Adam fixed me a
martini with two toothpicks and six olives. I don't
usually drink anything more alcoholic than wine because

43

I don't like getting drunk. But I do like olives. Olive oil is good for you. Roger just wanted a beer, like always.

We took our drinks out to the deck, and Adam introduced us to Tom and Juanita Hendrix, who live in apartment G, next to Richard. Tom and Juanita have lived here a long time. They even remember when practically everybody was a hippie, like them, instead of gay.

The fireworks show didn't start on time but I didn't care. I was feeling very comfy there on Adam's deck, sipping my martini and eating my olives. I could hear voices, the murmur of people having a good time at a party, and I smiled, picturing Pamela Parker's guests happily waving their little flags around on her deck. I wondered if Pamela could see the flags waving. Peter told me the reason she doesn't drive is that she can't see well enough to get a drivers' license, even with glasses.

And then it was just one voice I was hearing. Somebody was yelling and screaming so loud you would think it was a 911 emergency. The noise was coming from the driveway, in front of Richard's apartment, so we all ran to Adam's front door to see what was going on.

44

"Day-am! Is that some tiger got loose from the zoo, or what?" Adam wanted to know.

But it wasn't a tiger. It was Evonna. And she was throwing things all over the driveway, dishes and pots and pans and pillows and blankets, screaming like the crazy person she is the whole time. Then she got into her SUV, which was parked right there with the engine running, and, gunning the motor, ran over the pile of stuff scattered on the driveway. Then she put the car in reverse and ran over everything again. The car window was open and we could hear her laughing hysterically. Then Richard was walking toward the car.

"What the hell are you doing?" he yelled. But it was obvious what she was doing. She was destroying as many of Richard's belongings as she could.

He kept yelling. "Stop it, Evonna! I never said, I never told you…"

The car wasn't moving now. But Evonna hadn't gotten out. If she was crying, we couldn't hear her. By the time the official fireworks show started, Evonna had been taken away in a police car, and Richard, trying to look like his usual dignified self, was returning what hadn't been broken or totally flattened to its rightful

45

place in his apartment.   He refused to let anybody help him, and he ignored us when we tried to tell him how awful we thought it was for Evonna to do that.

Later on, I told Adam about having dinner with Evonna and how she told me her secret.

"I promised not to tell anybody, Adam, but now it seems like somebody besides me should know. Do you think she was just making it up about Richard asking her to marry him?"

"I purely don't know, Miss Nancy. But it's a sure thing them two is not getting hitched any time soon. She sure was hell bent on ruining as much of his goods as she could. She was so mad I bet she could've bit the head off a nail. And I reckon we have not heard the end of this story yet."

When we finally did get to see the fireworks show, put on by the Chamber of Commerce at great expense, we were not disappointed. The thing is, when they shoot the fireworks off from your very own beach, it seems like you can catch the lights as they fall toward the ground and it feels like you are a princess who can afford to buy even the stars in the sky.

46

Sometimes I wish everybody could live in California, especially Emma.

JUST A CAT

I feel sad today because Adam's cat, Booker T.,
died. He was just a cat, but I liked him. He had this cute
way of looking right at you and putting his front paw out
as if he wanted to shake hands. And he started purring
as soon as you said, "Hi, Booker T." He was black all
over, except for some gray whiskers. And he wasn't very
big. I think he was real old. I never saw him run, and he
walked sometimes like his legs were hurting him.

I was the one who found him. He was lying in the
street in front of Adam's house, and at first I thought he
was soaking up the sunshine like he liked to do, but he
was just too still. And flies were buzzing around him.

Adam is gone for the weekend, so I called Richard,
and he came right away. He was carrying a cardboard
box. Juanita saw us from her front window and brought
a black cloth to wrap Booker T. in and some roses from
her deck to put on top of him. She added a couple of
buds of pot "to make his journey easier," she said.

Richard opened Adam's front door with his
master key, and we put the box in the living room.

"Bye, Booker T.," I said. "You were a nice cat, and I am so glad I got to know you."

"Bye, buddy," Richard added, his head bowed. "I will miss you."

I hope Adam gets home pretty soon because it's really going to smell bad in there after awhile. Maybe we should have put Booker T. in an ice chest with lots of ice. Maybe we still can if Adam isn't home by tomorrow morning.

I wonder if animals have souls, all animals, I mean. But how can we eat them, then? Is one little humming bird or even one little caterpillar just as important to God as I am?

BLUE LOUIE

MEMORANDUM

To: All Tenants
From: Richard Stamp
RE: Miscellaneous Announcements
Date: August 5th, 2008

Beginning August 30th, pool use will be restricted to weekends, except for special requests, such as birthday parties, etc. Hot tub is as usual.

Some residents are making a habit of calling me after I have quit work for the day. This is not appropriate. If you have a true emergency, please call 911. Otherwise, it can wait until morning, with the exception of broken water pipes, plumbing overflows and fires. Please exercise care and diligence to nip such serious-type problems in the bud. Or at least try to notice them before five p.m.

Also, I am taking this opportunity to remind everybody that making sure the Cottages is a safe and secure place for our valued residents is a necessary part of my job. It would be easier if people would stop opening their doors to every riff-raff street person that wanders in.

Another important reminder: As you all know, our national elections are coming up in

November. Be sure you are properly registered to vote. We need all the Democrats we can get.

Yours truly,
R. Stamp, G.M.

I think I'll write Richard a memo back because he is just wrong about us not calling him after five p.m. He gets off work then, but he is supposed to be on call all the time. That's why he lives here instead of somewhere else. I think it says so in my rental agreement.

I wonder why Richard is so touchy lately. Maybe it's because of Evonna. A couple of days ago I heard our General Manager yelling, "Shut up!" at a little black bird that was chirping away on a telephone wire by the laundry room. It was kind of funny, actually, because the bird did shut up. But what isn't funny is that Richard has been served with a paper that says he has to defend himself in small claims court against 'one Miss Evonna Courtland.' Gosh, you would think it would be the other way around. Of course, Evonna isn't living here anymore. She got a thirty-day notice to move out after she ran over Richard's stuff on the Fourth of July. But Adam was right, I guess, when he said we haven't heard the end of the Richard and Evonna story yet.

I don't know if the election will change anything. I hope it will because I just love Mr. Obama. We're all blue here in Riverville, at least everybody I've talked to is. I don't personally know anyone who voted for President Bush. I don't hate our President, though; I'm sure he is doing the best he can.

I think the riff-raff Richard is talking about is Blue Louie. We don't call him Blue because of politics. I don't think he's attached to any political group. He's just weird. The first time I saw him I thought he lived here at the Cottages and that therefore maybe I shouldn't live here. Now I know better. He drives Richard crazy, coming over from wherever he does live all the time and knocking on people's doors. Richard is really big on security, and so is Mister D. That's why we have a front gate that gets locked at night if Jimmy remembers to do it when he goes home after work.

I don't know what Blue Louie's real name is. We call him that because he dyes his hair manic-panic blue and makes it all spiky with gel. He's not very big, in fact he's real skinny and not as tall as me, but he has a wild look in his eyes that makes him a scary sight standing on your front porch and telling you Jesus is dead, but it's okay because Jesus loves you and so does Louie, and do you have a couple of bucks?

Most people give him money. I know I do, just to get rid of him. But why do we have people like that? Why can't we find somewhere to put them so they can be safe and we can be safe, too? Juanita invites Louie in and gives him food, which I do not think is a good idea. What if he doesn't leave when you ask him to?

I do believe Jesus loves us, and I think He would feel right at home in Riverville. Everywhere you go you hear people, well, usually it's girls, saying, "Bye, Hon, love you." In the grocery store, on the street, in the post office. Sometimes they're even yelling it across the parking lot in front of that bar they call Spank's.

I don't know why we have such a loving population. Maybe it's because the Sisters of Perpetual Indulgence set such a good example. The Sisters are actually men who dress up like women and put on fund-raising events. Last year, they raised over $12,000 at their bingo games and gave it all away to various deserving people such as Riverville Grammar School and the Senior Center and even a little boy for his Four-H project.

Adam told me the Sisters got written up once in the newspaper for their giving ways. I think it was on the TV news, too. What they did was pay for a sound system for the Save the Eagles people so the baby birds could hear a pretend mother eagle voice and try harder to get out of their shells. At first it was just an experiment. But then it actually worked. Now there are little eagles flying all over the place, according to Adam.

YOURS TRULY, JOHN DE ANGELO

NOTICE TO ALL TENANTS:

From: John De Angelo, Smoke Hill Cottages
Date: Saturday, August 23rd

Hello Everyone,
 As some of you know, I returned from Europe just yesterday. Upon arriving home I found that our General Manager, Richard Stamp, had left on an emergency basis to be with his brother in Idaho who is very sick. If Richard were here he would be writing this. As it is, the unpleasant duty falls upon me.
 It saddens me to think that anyone would take advantage of the General Manager's absence to ignore one of our most important safety rules, namely the rule about not using firearms anywhere on the premises. Whoever put several dozen trout from the river in the swimming pool and then shot at them, probably with a pellet gun, while they were swimming around should be ashamed. The fish have been removed, but it is going to cost me at least twelve hundred dollars to drain the pool and redo the plaster.
 On a happier note, Miss Pamela Parker wishes to thank our General Manager for successfully connecting her apartment to Peter Jensen's earlier this month.

   Yours truly,
   John De Angelo

57

So now Mister D has to re-plaster the pool. It needed re-plastering anyway. But that was really a sick thing to do, putting all those little fish in the pool. They were probably already half dead from the chlorine even before they got shot. Other stuff is happening, too. Juanita told me that yesterday Mrs. Carmichael nearly fell down on the way to the laundry room because somebody put croquet wickets between the stones of the walkway. Of course, Richard, when he gets back from Idaho, will think Bobby did that and put the trout in the pool, too. But I don't know. How much grief can one little boy cause all by himself?

At least Bobby wasn't the one who set off the firecrackers on Mr. D's front porch on the Fourth of July. That turned out to be Mr. D's own grandson who was visiting here with his mom at the time. Not that Bobby wouldn't do something like that if he had the chance.

Now part of the wall between Pamela's living room and Peter's is missing, and Pamela has a huge space for entertaining her friends, while Peter has just his little kitchen and his bedroom and bathroom left. I know Peter said okay to putting a hole in the wall because he likes the idea of having Pamela pay his rent, which she said she would do if he would agree to give up his living room. But I feel sorry for him. Now how is he going to have any privacy?

I think I'll see if he wants to go to the Sisters of Perpetual Indulgence bingo game with me tonight, just Peter and me, because Roger wants to watch the boring baseball game. I hate baseball. If Roger and me ever get married we are going to have two TVs.

FREE STUFF

MEMORANDUM

To: All Tenants
From: Richard Stamp
Date: September 16th, 2008
RE: Changed hot tub hours

Dear Residents,

As you know, Mister De Angelo has been trying to
cut expenses where possible since he doesn't want
to inconvenience people by raising their rents.
Therefore, beginning next week hot tub use will be
restricted to Tuesday and Thursday between noon
and two p.m. and weekends and holidays from six
p.m. to nine p.m.

A Reminder: Please note that Thursday is my day
off. I would greatly appreciate it if you would try
not to be in need of assistance on Thursdays.

> Thank you,
> Richard Stamp,
> General Manager

Well, if Mr. D raises my rent I'm out of here. I can
hardly afford it as it is. I don't really use the hot tub that

much, but some people do. They're not going to like the new hours. And what are we supposed to do if we need help and it just happens to be Thursday?

Last Saturday night, Roger wanted to watch baseball, and Peter had to take Pamela to her daughter's house in the city after he got off work. I didn't want to go to the Sisters' bingo game all by myself, so I asked Juanita and Tom Hendrix if they wanted to go with me, which they did.

The thing about the Sisters' bingo games is they're very popular. You have to go early and stand in line if you want to get a good seat, or even any seat at all. Well, we did stand in line long enough to get the good seats, and it was already a lot of fun, even before the bingo games started. The Sisters were all dressed up in high heels and sparkly dresses, and were talking to people and sitting on guys' laps and handing out raffle tickets. One of them announced that you had to be over eighteen to play, and no alcohol was allowed except if it was already inside you. That got a big laugh. Then she said she wanted to give out a lot of free stuff, and everybody started yelling, "Free stuff, free stuff!" and stamping their feet.

The first raffle ticket winner was a woman sitting at our table. She won a pedicure at the nail salon on Main Street. The second winner was another woman, and she won a free car wash. I was thinking these were pretty good prizes and I hoped I would win something.

Then the first bingo game got under way. I had to really concentrate to keep up because I'm not used to playing bingo and Juanita was chewing gum and kept popping it. It was annoying and I wished she would stop doing it.

"Bingo!" somebody yelled. Tom was wadding up his used bingo cards, which were not really cards, just sheets of paper. So I did the same. Then wads were flying all over the room, like we were back in junior high school again. I threw mine at a cute guy at the table next to ours. But he didn't notice me.

The Sister in the pink dress, I think her name is Wanda, presented the bingo person with one hundred dollars. And then it was back to free stuff again. Only Juanita was yelling, "Free shit." Our whole table started laughing and then they were yelling it, too. Pretty soon everybody was yelling, "Free shit," me included. My grandma always said, a lady is a lady, regardless. So I was glad she wasn't there to hear me. I don't think my grandma ever attended any events, though, where it was hard to tell who was a lady and who was just pretending to be one for the sake of charity.

Two more winners, and I still wasn't one of them. The next game was explained to us by another one of the Sisters. What we had to do, she said, was get all of the numbers around the free space in the middle of our cards.

"This is known as a little mouth," she said. But there was a catch. If we managed to get them all, we had to yell out, "I have a little mouth," instead of "Bingo!"

I thought it would be easy to win this game, but I was wrong. We played for what seemed like forever before someone finally shouted, "Bingo!"

Oh-oh, I thought. He's in trouble because he didn't do it right. He was supposed to say that other thing.

Well, sure enough, suddenly everybody was real quiet and Wanda walked in her high heels over to where the guilty person was sitting.

"Come with me," she said to him. And when they reached the front of the room she asked him to take his shirt off, which he did, blushing. Then music like they play when somebody does a striptease act started up, and 'Mister Bingo,' which Wanda said was his new name, danced in a klutzy kind of way up and down the aisles between the tables. Wanda followed him with a big paper sack and invited us all to donate a dollar for the privilege of decorating Mister Bingo's bare chest with our daubers. I donated three dollars for Juanita and Tom and myself. That was the least I could do, since it was all for charity.

By the time we got to the last bingo game I was ready to call it quits, even though there was still more free stuff to win. Juanita was popping her gum again and I was worried I might call out bingo before I actually had all the numbers. Tom says the Sisters spank people with a wooden paddle when they call out bingo and don't really have one, right there in front of all those people. I don't know if that's true. I just know I would about die if I had to go to the front of the room and get spanked or if I had to dance around and let people mark me up with their daubers. Tom says the Sisters aren't embarrassing to everybody though. He doesn't think they would pick on a really shy person. And anyway, it's all in fun, like the make-up and the high heels, all for the sake of Riverville's fire department and other needy groups.

We played the last game, then walked back to the Cottages. The front gate was open, not locked like it usually is so late at night.

"Somebody's been here who doesn't belong here," Tom said. "Probably came in over the top of the fence and opened the gate from the inside when he went back out."

"Or else, Jimmy forgot to lock up," Juanita said.

When I came up to my front door I saw that there were three more pieces of spearmint gum on my welcome mat.

PETER'S NIGHT OUT

MEMORANDUM

To: All Tenants
From: Richard Stamp
Date: October 7th, 2008
RE: Parking rules and neighborhood safety
considerations

Greetings,

Mr. De Angelo has noticed that the handicap
parking spaces are almost never available for
people with true handicaps or for his friends, who
now have to park on the street. This is because
some of you are allowing your own un-
handicapped friends to park there. The handicap
spaces are reserved for people with official DMV
placards and/or Mr. De Angelo's invited guests
only.

Also: It has been brought to my attention that one
of our residents had a bit too much to drink at a
local watering hole last Friday evening and
thought it would be a good idea to convert his
apartment to a homeless shelter for the night.
Please don't do this. It makes it very difficult to
maintain a proper level of security.

Richard Stamp,
General Manager

What we really need around here is guest parking. Then people wouldn't have to park in the handicap spaces.

I don't think Richard knows I was with the guilty party when he had too much to drink. I really like to go out with Peter. He's a lot of fun. Roger can be fun, too, when he wants to be, but a lot of the time he would rather be watching TV than going out.

Anyway, last Friday night Peter asked me if I wanted to hang out with him at Spank's for a while after work. I like going to Spank's because it's a gay bar and usually I get to be the only girl there, which is cool. Besides that, everybody knows everybody else who goes there, so it feels real friendly.

When we got to Spank's we saw that Adam was there, so we sat down next to him.

"First round's on me," Adam announced.

"In that case, I'll have a double gin and tonic with a vodka chaser," Peter said.

I looked at him. "A vodka chaser? Peter, what's wrong with you?"

"I'm going to drive Pamela's car off a cliff and see if it's true you can open the door and jump out at the last minute and not get hurt, like in the movies."

I laughed. "Well, that's just silly, Peter. You would never do that. Why would you want to wreck Pamela's car, anyway?"

"Because I'm tired of driving her around in it. And not being able to smoke pot anymore, now that a chunk of the wall between our two apartments is missing." Peter chug-a-lugged his double shot with the vodka chaser and ordered another one.

"And now she wants me to dye my hair black and dress up like Count Dracula."

I laughed. Peter is as blond as you can get. I couldn't imagine him with black hair.

"Why does she want you to look like that?" I asked.

"Because she's having her book club over next Wednesday, you know, the Big Bottom Valley Ladies' Book Club, and she thinks it would be 'adorable' if I dressed up like Dracula and scared them. They just finished reading a book about vampires, and Pamela can't wait to serve them Bloody Mary's on the back deck while I hide in the bushes waiting for the perfect moment to jump out and yell 'boo,' or whatever it is vampires yell."

Adam was looking at Peter and nodding his head.

"In Tennessee, especially around Nashville, there's a lot of folks who will tell you they've seen vampires," he said. "My cousin, Jeanie Jo, swears she got sucked near dry by one a few years back."

"But Adam, vampires aren't real," I protested. "They just made them up to scare little kids."

"Well, let me tell you something, Miss Nancy Lou. In Tennessee, some folks will not go out at night when they believe vampires are about, and that's the truth."

I decided to let it go. It didn't seem worth arguing about. But where was Peter? All of a sudden I noticed he wasn't sitting by me. Then I saw him and heard him at the same time. He was on his way out of the bar, and seemed to be headed for the hot tub at the hotel next door. Why else would he take off all his clothes, except for his flip-flops? He was yelling something about Pamela being a hopeless, incurable control freak.

Of course, the bar manager caught up with Peter real quick. He threw a towel around him, handed him his clothes and tried to send him home in a cab. But Peter, complaining loudly about being treated like a

70

common drunk, insisted on walking. I didn't really want to walk with him, so I started off in the opposite direction. I figured I could double back after a few minutes and not be in danger of catching up with my embarrassing friend.

A little while after I got home, there he was, still wrapped in the towel, knocking at my door. He had half a dozen street people with him, and he had hold of the end of a dog leash. On the other end of the leash was the biggest Great Dane I personally have ever seen, and Blue Louie was standing on the other side of the dog, grinning at me.

"These nice people have kindly escorted me home," Peter said thickly. "And this is their mascot, Big Trouble. We are all going to have a little party and then they are going to spend the night. Would you care to join us?"

I told him no, shook hands with Peter's new friends and nodded hello to Louie. Then I waved goodbye and shut and locked my door. I wondered if I should call Richard. But then I remembered that Adam left Spank's before we did. I called him and told him about the party plans, and he went over to Peter's to check things out. As soon as he saw what was going on, he talked everybody into leaving (except the party host, of course, who was passed out on Pamela's living room couch). They were only too happy to leave, in fact, after Adam told them the sheriff was on his way to make sure everything was properly safe and law-abiding in the neighborhood.

After Adam got back to his apartment, he called to tell me not to worry because the street people had left and Peter was safely tucked into bed.

"Miss Pamela didn't even wake up," he said. "I reckon she had her bedroom door closed."

I went to bed then, but I just couldn't seem to get to sleep. I was feeling lonesome. It's been a long time since I've talked to Emma, I thought. I wonder how she is. I opened up my laptop and began typing.

'Emma, how come I haven't heard from you. Maybe now it's you who doesn't remember me.

'I have so much to tell you. Roger and me are seeing each other a lot. Last week he took me to meet his family in Milpitas, which is a little town, or actually not so little, near San Francisco. His Mom fixed dinner for

72

us, and his two brothers and their wives came over. Roger's dad is a partner in a hardware store, and the brothers work there, too. One of the wives works in a dentist's office and the other one stays home because she has a two-year-old and a baby. I felt right at home with Roger's family. They are just like any regular family in Oklahoma.

'Emma, you wouldn't believe some of the stuff that happens around here. Tonight I had a date with Peter, the guy who works at the restaurant with me, I think I told you about him already. It was okay with Roger because he knows Peter is gay. Anyhow, Peter got carried away and took all his clothes off, right there in front of everybody at Spank's bar. I was amazed, and so was everybody else. Even in California people don't take all their clothes off in public, unless it's a nude beach or they're soaking in a hot tub.

I think I'll come home for Thanksgiving.

Nancy'

THE BIG BOTTOM LADIES

MEMORANDUM

To: All Residents
From: Richard Stamp
Date: November 4th, 2008

Dear Residents,

Please, when you are planning a party or other special event, be considerate of your neighbors. The incident last Wednesday evening was most unfortunate. As I'm sure you all know by now, Betty Carmichael had to be taken to the emergency room after falling as she attempted to escape what she believed to be some kind of monster. She's okay now, but she could have suffered a serious injury, and Mr. De Angelo would not like to think that we might be sued because of what could be perceived as negligence on our part as owners and managers of the Cottages.

Sincerely,
Your General Manager, UFN

'UFN?' What's that supposed to mean, I wonder?

The unfortunate incident Richard is talking about happened right in front of my apartment. Wednesday is

75

when Pamela Parker's book club, The Big Bottom Valley Ladies, meets, and last Wednesday it was Pamela's turn to have them at her place. I knew she was planning for Peter to dress up like a vampire and scare the ladies as they were sipping their cocktails on the back deck. That's because the book club just finished reading the story of Count Dracula, and Pamela, according to Peter, likes to outdo the other book club members by having special effects when the meeting is at her apartment. You would think the ladies would meet at the library, read their books, talk about them, and then just go home. But instead they have these elaborate dinners and entertainments at each other's houses. Pamela told Peter they have been meeting for a long time, so I guess they would all be bored to death by now if they acted like a normal book club.

Anyhow, I really don't know why Peter doesn't just say no when Pamela asks him to do these ridiculous things. It would have been okay, I guess, if it hadn't been starting to get dark already and if Peter had waited until the book club ladies were sitting on Pamela's back deck before going outside in his vampire get-up. But he just couldn't wait to show me how he looked with his cape and his fangs, so he decided to walk over to my apartment before showing up at the book club meeting.

He never made it to my apartment. Little Mrs. Carmichael, who was standing on her front porch, trying to find where in her purse she had put her door key, saw Peter crossing the street, flapping like a bat and swooping, or at least trying to swoop, as he rehearsed his vampire moves, and it seemed to her that this giant black fly, or whatever it was, was heading straight for her.

Adam was just walking in through the front gate after downing a couple of beers at Spank's when Mrs. Carmichael screamed and started running toward Richard's apartment. Well, of course Adam, of all people, would have to be there right then. When he saw Mrs. C running away and a monster in a black cape coming after her, he did the gentlemanly thing and came to Mrs. C's rescue. Poor Peter. Adam's not any bigger than he is, but Adam knows how to tackle a person. He told me once that he played football in tenth grade and was named tenth grade player of the year. He knocked Peter to the ground and then sat on him, yelling obscenities and threatening to keep him pinned there all night long.

Right about then several of the Big Bottom ladies walked through the front gate on their way to Pamela's. It looked to them like Adam was attacking an innocent child in some kind of Halloween costume, even though Halloween was still a couple of days off, and so one of them called the police on her cell phone. Pamela, when she noticed Peter seemed to be missing and her ladies seemed to be arriving late, came out of her apartment to see what was the matter. By then Adam realized it was Peter he had pinned to the ground, and said,

"Shoot. I plumb forgot you was fixin' up fer Miss Pamela's book club. Sorry, y'all. I thought you was real."

The police arrived and called for an ambulance to take Mrs. C, who could barely walk, to the emergency room to see if her ankle was just sprained or was maybe broken. Adam was limping, too, but insisted he was perfectly fine. Peter had a bloody nose and a broken fang.

So Pamela didn't get to surprise her ladies. Peter was in no mood to jump out of the bushes and scare them by then. Besides, the ladies already knew it was just Peter.

I think I'll ask Richard why he signed his memo, 'Your General Manager, UFN.' And I think I'll ask him if Evonna is still suing him in small claims court and if he wants any of us to go with him and be witnesses. Peter would go, and Tom and Juanita, and probably Adam. But I still don't know what Evonna is claiming Richard did that was so awful.

THE PARADE OF LIGHTS

I went home to Oklahoma for Thanksgiving, and I felt like I didn't belong there anymore. I played tag football with my cousins like always, but it didn't seem the same. Even Mom's homemade biscuits just didn't taste like they used to. Maybe I'd rather have sourdough now. Maybe I really am starting to be a California girl. I should feel happy, I guess. But how does a person know if they're happy, I wonder. I mean, happy, not just ecstatic from having sex or something.

I saw Emma while I was in Oklahoma. I showed her some pictures of Wanda and the other Sisters, all dressed up for charity, and she was amazed. But she still doesn't think she would like to actually see them in person. And she says she doesn't care if she never plays bingo. Emma is so backward.

I flew back to California on December 1st. People in Riverville are starting to worry because it has hardly rained at all so far this winter. Nobody has ever seen the river this low in December.

It was good that it wasn't raining last Saturday night, though, because that's when we had the parade of lights. The Chamber of Commerce puts on the parade, just like they put on the fireworks show on the Fourth of July. I wonder where they get the money to do these things. Maybe the Sisters help out. Anyway, I took Saturday night off from work. It's easier to get weekends off now that Joe's wife is working at the restaurant. She says she likes to work weekends because the tips are good, but I think she just wants to keep an eye on Joe. He comes on to people when she isn't there.

A little before dark, Roger and me walked downtown and found ourselves a good place to watch the parade, right between the tackle shop and the pizza place. We could see Pamela and Peter across the street. Peter was carrying a couple of folding chairs.

"Pamela thinks of everything," I said to Roger. "I wish we'd thought to bring chairs."

At first it didn't look like the parade was going to amount to much, just a few kids marching and playing their band instruments, not very well. Then a couple of horses with their bridles and saddles lit up. But when the floats started coming by it was a different story. I could hardly believe how many lights were decorating some of those trucks, especially the fire trucks, and all battery operated, of course. It was awesome.

I noticed there were a lot of kids watching the parade. Most of the winter events in Riverville cater more to adults. The leather contests, for example. I asked Roger what they do at those contests, and he said he wouldn't tell me because I might be shocked. Actually, Roger has never been to a leather event and doesn't have the faintest idea what they do there. So that makes two of us.

The parade lasted less than an hour, which was long enough, since the nights are so chilly now.

After the parade was over I walked back to the Cottages alone. Roger wanted to have a couple of beers with his friends at the Dugout.

When I came through the front gate I saw that Mrs. Carmichael's lights were on, so I knocked on her front door.

"Who is it?" she asked.

"Nancy, Mrs. Carmichael."

She opened the door. "Oh, I'm so glad to see you, dear. And how was the parade?"

I told her about the marching kids and the horses and the gorgeous floats.

"Was Bobby in the parade?"

"No, Ma'am," I said. "At least not that I could see."

"Well, that little dickens told me he was going to be Santa Claus and ride on the same float as the parade princess."

I laughed. "I don't think there even was a parade princess, Mrs. Carmichael."

"I worry about that boy, Nancy. His mother yells at him. And his father, when he picks him up for school in the morning, yells at both of them and calls them dirt. Some mornings, Bobby's father never shows up and Bobby doesn't go to school. It's not a good thing when young people have too much time on their hands."

Mrs. Carmichael fixed me some hot chocolate, and we sat on her couch and talked a while longer. I thought I saw something run across her kitchen floor, maybe a little mouse, but I wasn't sure. I decided not to tell her.

I was thinking about Bobby and remembering how he told me, when I first met him by the pool: "Us

MacKenzies is nuthin' but trouble. My daddy says we's the most trouble this shitty town has ever seen."

Tomorrow I'm going to Adam's church with him. I don't usually attend church. I do believe in God, but I don't much believe in churches. All they seem to do is pick on each other. But Adam says his church is different.

MEMORANDUM

To: All Tenants with porches and/or decks
From: Richard
Date: December 16th, 2008
RE: Winter Safety

Winter has arrived, and we are experiencing some unusually cold weather. Please be careful when walking on your porches and/or decks. If there is ice, try to avoid it, as ice can be very slippery. If you have any salt or sand, you can apply such substances to cut down on slipperiness. Otherwise, try not to walk on your porches and/or decks until the sun has been out long enough to melt any accumulated ice. We care about your safety.

The holidays will be here before we know it. Mr. De Angelo and I would like to take this opportunity to wish you all a very merry Christmas and a happy new year.

>   Sincerely,
>   Richard Stamp,
>   Manager, The Cottages

Just, 'Manager, The Cottages?' No 'UFN?' I guess Mr. D is worrying again about being sued. That must be why Richard is warning us about slipping and sliding around on our decks.

I went to church in Hennington, which is about fifteen miles away, with Adam on Sunday. Adam's church calls itself Christian but believes in everything else, too, just to be on the safe side. When it's time to celebrate Hanukkah with the Jewish people, they do, and when it's time to bless the animals with the Buddhists, they do, which is something I like because I really do think animals have souls. Adam says the church even has a drive thru for grumpy pets on animal blessing day.

Adam knocked on my door about nine-thirty a.m. on Sunday, and we drove over to Hennington. The church didn't look much like one. I think it was once a bowling alley or something that the congregation moved to when they got too big for the original church building. And boy, was it cold in there.

We sat up near the front where we could see everything that went on. I looked around. I was expecting to see a bunch of old people, but actually most everybody was pretty young. Then the music started,

88

rock-n-roll gospel, I guess you'd call it. People were getting in the mood with the music, clapping their hands and even getting out of their seats and dancing around.

After a few minutes, the music stopped and the pastor came up to the microphone. He was young, too, probably not thirty yet.

"Good morning!" he yelled so loud it made me jump.

"Good morning!" everybody yelled back.

"Are you ready to let change happen in your life?"

"Yes!" we shouted, enthusiastically.

"Then I want you to get out there and push the envelope, dare to do, think success, be outrageous for God."

Then he told us a story about Jesus and how he stood up to the people in power at that time, and how beloved he has become through the ages because of daring to question the way things were. I was thinking that one of the results of Jesus standing up to the people in power was that he got killed, but I did like what the pastor said next.

"I want all of you to write down a list of things you have been meaning to do and just haven't gotten around to, and I want you to do one thing every day this next week. Do you have a friend you're out of touch with? Call that friend. Are you so stuck on chocolate ice cream you can't give mango a try? Try it."

By the time the pastor finished his talk I was totally inspired. And when the music started up again, I was one of the people who were dancing.

After we got back to the Cottages, I thanked Adam for taking me to his church and gave him a great big hug. He smiled and said he would be pleased to take me anytime I wanted to go.

When I walked through the front door of my apartment the phone was ringing. I picked it up and heard Peter on the other end.

"Hey, Nan, how about going to the casino?" he asked. "Pamela just paid me and all three dollars are burning a hole in my pocket."

"I'd love to go to the casino, Peter," I told him. "I'll drive if you want."

So I grabbed my wallet and keys and met Peter in the parking lot.

"Did you know I went to church with Adam this morning, Peter?"

90

"Whatever for?" was his response.

"Well, I just thought it would be interesting, that's all."

"And was it?"

"Oh my gosh, you wouldn't believe how fired up everybody got, me included. The pastor said we should all do something kind or something brave every day for a week. That way we could know we were following in Jesus' outrageous footsteps."

"Why would you want to do that?"

"Why wouldn't I? Peter, I want to be the kind of person who dares to push the envelope, like the pastor said. That's why I came to California in the first place."

"Well, Nancy, if you really want to be outrageous, why don't you do the pastor's homework assignment all on the same day, all day long. That way you won't have to worry about it the rest of the week. Doesn't that sound like fun?"

It did sound like fun, especially if Peter would help me. He said he would be honored to help, and we made a date for next Wednesday, which I have off from work, it being such a slow time of year for the restaurant.

I was lucky at the casino, probably due to my new church-going ways. But Peter lost a lot, not just three dollars, and we came home early.

"What time Wednesday?" I asked.

"How about noon?"

"That seems kind of late, Peter. How about ten thirty?"

"Okay, eleven it is."

I nodded and smiled. I know how much Peter hates to get out of bed in the morning.

On the way back to my apartment I noticed there was a light on in the office. Richard's working late, I thought. Or Mr. D. is. I knocked on the door.

"Come in," Richard answered. He was sitting at his desk, but he didn't have his computer turned on.

"I have a question for you, Richard, actually two," I said. "If you're not too busy."

"Yes?"

"What does UFN stand for?"

"Damned if I know."

"But that's how you signed your memo, the one about Mrs. Carmichael having to go to the emergency room: 'Richard Stamp, General Manager UFN.'"

"Oh. That stands for until further notice. I was thinking about quitting. I still am."

"Please don't do that, Richard. What would we do without you?" I was alarmed. Mr. D is practically never here, and Jimmy is good at fixing things, but I don't think he would like having to work in the office.

"Thanks for the vote of confidence, Nancy. It's just that I get discouraged sometimes." He was looking down at some kind of document, the court summons, I guessed.

"My second question is when do you have to go to court?"

He looked a little irritated, like maybe he didn't think it was any of my business. But then he said, "I'm supposed to show up next Wednesday, but I'm going to ask for a postponement. Mr. D thinks that if we keep postponing the date, Evonna might get tired of waiting and just drop the whole thing."

I wanted to ask him what the whole thing was about because I still didn't know, but then he probably would think I was being too nosy. So I just said, "Oh," and let it go at that. I forgot to ask him if he wanted anybody to go to court with him.

OH, WHAT FUN

"How do you want to begin?" Peter asked when we met in the Cottages parking lot on Wednesday morning. For some reason he was carrying a life-sized cardboard paper doll that had practically nothing on.

"Well, I thought we could start by visiting Emma's Aunt Muriel, if she happens to be home, which I hope she isn't. Emma has been asking me to look her up, and I guess it would be a kind thing to do. She lives not too far from here, and I have her address."

Peter got a bungee cord out of the trunk of his Chevy Impala convertible and started to strap the paper doll to the front bumper.

"We are not taking that doll with us, " I told him. "She is totally not appropriate."

"I thought you wanted to be outrageous. I thought it would be fun to see people's reactions." Peter sounded a little testy, and I didn't want him to quit on me before we even got started. So I decided to compromise.

"Well, why don't we tie something else to the bumper?"

"Like what?"

"Like… " But I couldn't think of anything.

"You are just too new to this, Nan. You can't be outrageous and appropriate at the same time."

Then I had an idea. "How about if I go get the teddy bear Mom sent me, the one with the fishing pole and the wader boots? We could tie him to the bumper, or maybe to the hood."

"The bear's okay, I guess, but we need some fish, which I just happen to have, for him to be angling for. You go get your cute little bear, and I'll go get the fish."

When I got back with the teddy bear Peter was already wrapping a piece of twine, with bright orange gold fish knotted onto it, to the front bumper. The fish were plastic and had huge shiny black buttons for eyes. They were different sizes, but the biggest ones were nearly a foot long.

"Very colorful," I said. Gross, I was thinking.

Peter sat the bear up on the front of the hood and tied it down. Then we climbed into the car and headed for Muriel's.

"What are we going to do next, after we visit Emma's aunt?" Peter asked.

"I don't know. What do you think we should do?"

Peter pulled the car off the road and killed the engine. "Nancy, you have to have a plan. How are we going to be outrageous all day long if you don't even have a plan?"

So that's when we came up with our list of things to do, hopefully outrageously. We didn't consult God. Maybe we should have, now that I think about it.

Anyway, we found Emma's Aunt Muriel's house. But she wasn't home. At least I could tell Emma I did try to visit her. That brought us to number two on our to-do list: Walk around in a pasture where there are bulls. Peter headed out of town, and it wasn't long before we were out in the country, looking for cows. We turned off the main road and went down one country lane and then another and another. We didn't see any cows. But we did see lots of sheep.

"Why don't we just go talk to a few sheep and then go on to the next thing, number three, which is: Try a new flavor of ice cream?" I asked. I was having second thoughts about getting anywhere near a real bull in a real pasture with a barbed wire fence.

Peter looked over at me with his eyebrows raised, and then just kept driving. This is no fun, I thought. It was sometime after noon by then, and I hadn't eaten breakfast. Ice cream of any flavor was really sounding good, and hot chocolate was sounding even better, since it was the dead of winter and we were driving around in a convertible with the top down.

"Okay," Peter said finally. "You win. We'll just skip number two because I sure as hell am not going to talk to a bunch of sheep. But we should have lunch before we start sampling weird ice cream flavors, don't you think?"

He turned the car around and headed back toward town. After a few minutes we saw a roadside diner and decided to stop there.

The hostess showed us to our table. "This isn't even on our to-do list," Peter said, and laid a deck of cards down in front of me. "What do you say we play poker?"

"Okay." I emptied my coin purse on the table.

Between us, we had a lot of change, and in no time at all it was sitting in neat stacks next to our napkin-wrapped silverware.

"Dealer's choice," Peter said. "Okay?"

"Okay, but I get to deal first. Draw poker with deuces wild."

I dealt the cards.

"May I help you?" Peter asked the waitress when she came over to take our orders.

"Actually, I'm supposed to be helping you, I believe," she said, not sounding quite sure. "Have you decided...?"

"Yes, I've decided to bet fifty cents," Peter said, and showed her his cards, being careful not to let me see them.

"Are you planning to order something to eat?" she asked hopefully, looking at me and trying not to notice that Peter had gotten up from the table and was going around the diner showing everybody his cards.

"I think I'll just have a BLT on wheat," I told her. "I'm not sure what my friend wants."

"Cheeseburger!" Peter yelled from the other side of the room.

The waitress left and Peter came back and sat down. I saw his bet and raised him seventy-five cents. We kept on playing poker while the waitress brought our orders, filled our water glasses a couple of times, and finally left the bill on the table with two complimentary peppermints, all without a word, and averting her eyes, I suppose so she could truthfully say she had not seen any illegal activity happening at the diner. In case somebody asked.

In Hennington an hour later, we found a place with every ice cream flavor there is. I tried 'Gourmet Gunk,' which looked terrible, like a blob of grease with dirt sprinkled on it, but tasted really yummy, kind of like a chocolate milkshake but with more of a dark chocolate taste. Peter tried 'Pomegranate Pudding' which he said was way better than he thought it would be.

The next thing on our to-do list was: Visit a fortune-teller. Neither of us had ever been to a fortune-teller, but we thought we knew what to expect. We were wrong. Our fortune-teller, who was wearing a turban and shiny slippers that were too big for him, took our cell phones away from us when we came in to his "Palace of Mysteries," and disappeared for ten minutes.

100

"He seems kind of small, Peter," I said. "I think he's only twelve or thirteen years old."

"Sh. Don't talk," Peter whispered, pointing to the microphone only half hidden in the ceiling fan.

When our fortune-teller came back he could recite the names of practically everybody we knew, and a few of their phone numbers too, after reading his palms, not ours. He predicted we would have long and happy lives and many friends. He usually charged much more for his services, he said, but because we were such nice people he would charge us only fifty dollars. Each.

Peter laughed and handed him a twenty-dollar bill. Then he pressed his fingertips to his forehead and, trying to sound all solemn and magical, said,

"Young man, I predict you will have a long and happy life and a very lucrative career in either show business or banking."

When we got back in the car and checked our to-do list, we realized it was already getting late. We weren't going to be able to do it all.

"Let's pick one last thing," Peter suggested, "and leave the rest for another day. "Just close your eyes, then touch something on the list. Whatever you touch, that's what we'll do."

I closed my eyes and touched. "Oh-KAY," Peter said, trying to sound cheerful. "Picking up trash along the highway it is."

"But that's not a good thing to end with," I protested. "It would be a kind deed, but it won't be fun, and we don't even have any trash bags to put stuff in. Let me try again."

"Look, Nan, why don't we just take a couple of poor people to dinner, that's on the list, then call it quits." He grinned. "You can take me and I can take you. We're poor. What do you say?"

"Peter, that sounds boring."

"Boring? Me boring? I am a lot of things, Miss Walker, but I am NEVER boring. Maybe you would like me to take you home now, if you're so freaking bored. Or maybe.... It's just an idea...."

He looked at me. He was grinning again. "Maybe you would like to play like we are Thelma and Louise. That will definitely not be boring."

"Who are Thelma and Louise?"

"Characters in an old movie. Thelma, the good little housewife, and her girlfriend, Louise, decide to take

102

some time off from their boring, yes, I said boring, lives and go on a road trip. Talk about outrageous. Before the movie's over they're in so much trouble all they can think of to do is drive Louise's convertible, I think it was a Thunderbird, off a cliff into the Grand Canyon. Susan Sarandon played Louise; I can't remember who played Thelma, but she was tall. I remember that. So what do you think?"

"Okay," I said, "just as long as we don't really drive off a cliff."

Peter laughed. "Oh, don't be silly, girl. We're not going to drive off a cliff. I like my car too much. Who do you want to be, Thelma or Louise?"

"Well, you're the one driving the car. Why don't you be Louise?"

"Okay. Then you're the one who gets raped, and I'm the one who shoots the rapist dead."

"Oh, what fun," I said, not knowing what else to say.

"That's the spirit, luv," Peter said, and lit two cigarettes, one for him and one for me. "Put your feet up on the dash, Nan, and pretend you're wearing a pair of designer jeans instead of those cutesy capris, or whatever they are."

"Gauchos. From TJ Max."

We drove along, Peter smoking his cigarette and me just holding mine and trying not to choke on the smoke, waiting for something interesting to happen, and then it did. A truck driver passed us on the right and gave us the finger as he went by.

"Girlfriend," Peter said, "we are independent women and we are not going to let this go."

"No, we are not," I agreed, trying to sound like a cigarette smoking, unhappy housewife who was taking a road trip with her best friend.

We speeded up and cut in front of the truck. Then Peter slowed down so that the truck driver had to slow down too, unless he wanted to plow into us, which he probably did want to by then.

Peter glanced up at the rear view mirror. "He's talking on his cell phone, Nan, and he doesn't look happy. Let's see how he likes this." Peter began crossing back and forth between the lanes, doing a little dance with the car for the truck driver's benefit. I unfastened my seat belt, turned around in my seat, and stuck my tongue out. Then I took off my sweater and my t-shirt.

"Towanda!" I yelled.

Peter looked at me, amazed. "That's a different movie, Fried Green Tomatoes, I think," he said. Then he added, "I hope you're not going to take your bra off."

That's when the highway patrol pulled up behind us and blinked their lights at us to get off the road.

The officers were real polite.

"Mr. Jensen," one of them said after Peter showed him his registration and his drivers' license, "would you please exit your vehicle and demonstrate your ability to walk a straight line for us? And young lady, I am certainly glad to see that you have put your clothes back on."

I tried to explain to the officers about being outrageous for God, and how we were playing at being Thelma and Louise, but they acted like I was speaking a foreign language or something. One of them wrote out a ticket for 'driving too slow, driving in too many lanes, and driving with the intention of obstructing traffic.' Then he told us we were lucky he wasn't hauling us in to the station for being a danger to ourselves and other people.

We drove back to Riverville without saying much of anything. When we got home Peter untied my bear and handed it to me, minus one of its boots and with its fur going every which way from the wind.

"I guess we got a little carried away," I said. "I feel bad about the ticket. Let me help pay for it."

"That's okay, Nan. I was the one doing the driving. It's my ticket, not yours." He unwrapped the twine and what was left of the goldfish from the front bumper, and flashed me a big smile.

"Need anything at Safeway?" he asked. "I'm going to see if they have pomegranate ice cream."

A WHOLE SET OF DRUMS

I am just amazed. We all are, because Mrs. Carmichael bought a whole set of drums at the music store in Hennnington last week and had them delivered to her apartment. She's teaching Bobby how to play them. She says she learned 'the art of timpani' when she was in high school and played the kettledrum in the school orchestra. Richard is having a fit. But Mrs. C says it's for a good cause, keeping Bobby busy and out of trouble, and Richard should be glad about that. She has promised not to have any drum banging happening before nine in the morning or after nine at night. If it was anybody else we'd all be having a fit, but who can say no to Mrs. C? Adam bought everybody earplugs at the drug store and handed them out a couple of days ago. I can still hear the drums, especially the bass drum, thru the earplugs, but then I do live pretty close to Mrs. C, practically next door.

Emma called me a little while ago, and I told her I couldn't hear her very well because of the earplugs. She thought I was kidding. When I told her about the drums she said she didn't think that would be allowed in any apartment complex in Oklahoma. She has her own apartment in Landon now, so she thinks she knows about these things. She told me she was thinking of putting highlights in her hair. So I told her a lot of people in California are wearing earrings in their nipples. She said she thought that was totally disgusting. To tell the truth, I think it's kind of disgusting, too, but I might get a tattoo, maybe a rose and a couple of initials. Maybe RW, which stands for Roger Wills. And for sure I'm going to get some blond highlights put in my boring brown hair.

Christmas is next Thursday. Roger and me are going to Milpitas to be with his family. I think I'll call Mom and ask her for Grandma's recipe for Bethlehem star cookies. Maybe I'll make some fudge, too. Everybody likes fudge.

A DIFFERENT WORLD

Roger picked me up at noon on Christmas Day, almost an hour later than he said he was going to, and we headed for his parents' house in Milpitas. I had presents for the little kids, and cookies and fudge for everybody else. I was feeling happy and glad I had a warm and cozy place to go to for the holiday.

It seemed like everybody in the world was headed for Milpitas, though, there was that much traffic. We were on the road so long it felt like we must already be in Mexico. But we finally turned on to the street where Roger's parents live, and suddenly we were in a different world, a Walt Disney world, with reindeer and sleighs and little elves and fat, jolly Santas everywhere you looked, all lit up of course.

"Looks like the neighborhood just about bought everything Home Depot had to offer this year," Roger said. "Last year Mom and Dad won first place for Best Inflatable Art."

"Inflatable art? You mean they had to blow everything up?"

"It's not that hard, they have a pump. I always got to blow up Rudolph, when I lived at home."

"Have you ever been to Disneyland, Roger?"

"Nope."

"Me either. I'd like to go sometime."

"Yeah. Me too."

We parked in the driveway of his parents' house, and his dad came out to meet us.

"Merry Christmas!" he said. "You're late, Son."

"Traffic, Dad," Roger replied. He sounded annoyed.

His dad smiled at me and shrugged his shoulders.

When we were in the living room I looked around. There was a fire in the fireplace, a real one, not one of those gas ones. And stockings were hung on the mantle. And on the other side of the room was a Christmas tree, decorated with lights and just about everything else a person could think of to decorate a Christmas tree with. And of course there were presents underneath. Looks just like home, I thought.

Roger's dad announced, "Soup's on," and we sat down to dinner, roast beef and mashed potatoes. And Yorkshire pudding like my mom makes sometimes, and

110

which I really like. Roger's dad talked about how he didn't know what the world was coming to, what with global warming and a totally inexperienced person about to take over the presidency. Just like home, I thought again.

After dinner I helped Roger's mom clear the table and we all sat down again.

"We always play Pictionary after Christmas dinner," Roger's mom explained.

So we chose up sides and began to play. My side was ahead and it was my turn to draw. What I was trying to get them to guess was the song called *The Girl From Ipanema*. I didn't know that song, and I didn't have a clue where Ipanema was, but I did the best I could. I drew a stick figure with a skirt, and then I drew a map that looked kind of like the United States and arrows pointing from the map to the stick figure.

"Map girl! Weather girl!" Roger's sister shouted.

"It's a song, remember," Roger said. He wasn't even on our side; he was just trying to be helpful. I smiled at him.

I kept pointing to the map and then to the girl. Nothing.

Then Roger's mom said, "Draw something we can sound out, Nancy."

So I drew a big eye. But then I wondered if that's how you pronounce Ipanema, with an I sound at the beginning.

That's when Roger's brother yelled out, "I! I from! I Okie from Muskogee!"

Well, of course, everybody thought that was real funny. They just couldn't stop laughing, until they noticed I wasn't laughing with them. Then Roger's brother said he was sorry, he didn't mean to hurt my feelings, and I said it was okay. But it wasn't okay. One minute I was feeling like part of the family, and the next minute I was feeling like an alien.

Later, we opened presents. Everybody said the cookies I brought were delicious and the fudge about the best they had ever tasted. But nobody asked me for the cookie recipe, and I knew the fudge wasn't that great.

It was too late to call Mom after we got back. But I called her the next morning. She said it was snowing in Landon. And she said she missed me. I told her I missed her, too, and was wishing I could see some snow because it just didn't seem like Christmas without snow.

"Nancy, what's wrong? Are you sick? I read in the paper that a lot of people in California have the flu. You can always come home, you know. Dad and I will pay for the airplane tickets if you need us to."

She sounded worried.

"Mom, don't worry about me," I said. "I'm just fine, honest."

I wonder if other people lie to their mothers as much as I do.

ALICE COMES OUT OF THE CLOSET

MEMORANDUM

To: All Tenants
From: Richard Stamp
Date: January 6th, 2009

This is to let everybody know that annual safety inspections are about to begin, and we request that you advise us as to when would be a convenient time to have your apartment tested for safety, i.e. smoke detectors and drips, etc. We will also be replacing some of the doors that don't fit properly in order to (hopefully) reduce the incidence of door slamming.

Also, Mr. De Angelo wishes to thank all who participated in clean-up day. A great way to begin the year!

I guess most of you know by now that one of our residents, Adam Porter Jefferson won first place at the Closet Ball last weekend. Congratulations, Adam.

Sincerely
Richard Stamp,
General Manager

The holidays are over with, and I'm happy about that because I was getting so homesick for Oklahoma. But we always have a lot of stuff going on in Riverville. That's why I like it here, never a dull moment. In the summertime it's wall-to-wall tourists coming to see the rodeo and the blues festival and all the other tourist-type events we have, but in the winter there's a lot to do, too. The Sisters' bingo games are all year and the parade of lights is in December, and last weekend we had the closet ball. I wasn't going to go, but Roger talked me into it.

"Let's see what it's like, Honey," he said. "I hear it's a hoot. A bunch of guys get up on the stage and do a song or a couple of minutes of jokes or whatever, and then they dress up like women and do a whole different act."

So I went to the closet ball with Roger and therefore was late. Roger's always late for everything. It's so annoying. If we get married I'm just not going to put up with this stuff.

I guess we used to have a real nightclub in town, but it's been closed for a while, so the closet ball was held at Spank's, which is not nearly big enough. We had to sit in back of everybody else, and it was hard to tell what was going on. I could see there was a humongous box on the stage with a curtain across the front and 'closet' written in big letters above the curtain. One of the bingo Sisters was passing out jello shots. It was for charity, so I paid for two, one for Roger and one for me, and asked the Sister what was happening.

"Just about diddlysquat, Hon," she said. "The boys already did their guy acts. Now they are changing their clothes and putting on their make-up, getting ready to do their diva routines. Who knows how long that's going to take?" She rolled her eyes.

We downed our jello shots and waited. Roger was motioning to the Sister.

"I'm switching to beer," he said. "Jello doesn't belong in a bar." And then the announcer was introducing the first contestant, 'Amanda.' She stepped out of the closet onto the stage, and Roger began laughing. Because you could tell Amanda was really a boy, even though he had on long blond hair and a blue dress with matching high heels. For one thing, he had a dark beard, which did not go with the blond hair. He sang *I Feel Pretty* in a real deep voice, and everybody laughed, not just Roger. The second one was wearing even longer blond hair and a fabulous black evening dress, low cut to show off her pearls and her boobs. The announcer said her name was Alice.

"Wow, she's gorgeous," Roger said. "And she can really sing." She was singing *It Had To Be You,* but it was coming out more like "It hay-ad to Be You." And then she seemed to forget some of the words of the song, and I heard her say, "day-am." Suddenly I knew.

"Adam!" I gasped. "Is that you?"

Well, it was Adam and he totally won the contest. There were three more contestants, but none of them could sing like Adam. I had no clue he was so talented. I think I'll put a note on his door, and pretend it's from the people at American Idol, and they want him to audition.

After the closet ball Roger and me had a fight because he was walking like he says Adam and Peter walk. He doesn't get it that people can be straight or gay, and it doesn't matter, they're just who they are. I do like cuddling up with him in my bed. I just don't like being with him when he's acting like a jerk.

Emma e-mailed me this morning to tell me she is going to start taking classes at the J.C. in Landon. She says her mom and dad are going to help her pay for books and tuition.

I called her a little while ago and told her I thought it was great she was going to get a real education.

"How is Roger?" she asked me, like she was a mind reader or something. That's when I told her about our fight and how I'm going to let him know tonight that I just don't want to go out with him anymore if he's going to keep making fun of people.

"This is California, Emma, you know," I said.

"So what?"

"So I don't have to go out with him if I don't want to. I can just tell him to get lost."

"Well, yes, you can, but then who is going to take you to see stupid movies about giant worms? And who is going to take you bowling? And who is going to put his arms around you and kiss you and...?"

"Okay, Emma. Just shut up. Please."

But she kept right on talking. "I bet you anything he's going to send you flowers tomorrow," she said. "Guys always send flowers when they think you're going to break up with them. And don't tell me to shut up.

Please. It's not polite."

"Roger is not going to send me flowers," I said. "That's not his style."

PAMELA REQUESTS

I can't believe it's almost the end of January already. We still haven't had hardly any rain, but I guess they are getting plenty of it back east. And snow, too. I watched our new President be sworn in on TV, with Tom and Juanita last Tuesday. The people who were cheering when he gave his acceptance speech looked like they were about to freeze to death. It was that cold.

Pamela has invited us all to a party a week from Saturday. She is calling it a 'Willy' party, but it sounds to me like it's going to be an Oscar night party, whatever she wants to call it. Peter delivered the invitations yesterday dressed in a tuxedo and his flip-flops. The invitation says,

'Your presence is requested on Saturday, January 31st. Wear movie star attire and be prepared with some small bit of entertainment. Willies will be awarded to the most entertaining guests, and refreshments will be served by Mickey Mouse of Walt Disney fame.'

Poor Peter. Now I suppose he has to put on a pair of great big ears and pretend to be Mickey Mouse. And what am I going to put on? I don't have any real dressy clothes, or actually I do but they're in Oklahoma. I didn't think I would need them here.

Adam asked me this morning if I would be his date for Pamela's party, and I said yes. I don't really want to bring Roger, even if he did send me roses after I got mad at him, like Emma said he would. I think the party is supposed to be just for us neighbors. And anyhow, I'll see Roger on Sunday because we are going to a baseball game with his brothers then.

THE WILLIES

"Holy Moses, Miss Nancy," Adam said when we arrived at Pamela's for the party. "This looks mighty fancy." Pamela's car, shined up with wax, was parked in the Cottages driveway, in front of her apartment. And next to the car, on the passenger side, a red carpet was rolled out. Peter, who was wearing huge black ears and a tail, and had a big smudge on his nose, was taking pictures of people as they arrived, having them sit in the car, then get out and pose standing on the red carpet.

"Hi Nancy," he squeaked, trying to sound like a mouse.

"Hi," I squeaked back.

Then Adam and me stepped inside the apartment. Pamela's living room looked real festive. Gold and silver stars were tacked up on the walls, and there was a buffet table with platters of cheese and fruit and buckets of ice with wine and champagne. I bet Pamela invited more than just us neighbors to this party, I was thinking.

And then I saw the stage.

"Adam," I said, "somebody has set up a real stage. Look, in the corner. There's even a microphone and a spotlight."

I was suddenly remembering the piano recital when I was eight years old. I was all by myself on the stage, sitting at a piano, a huge baby grand. The spotlight was on me, and everybody was waiting, waiting.... but my fingers couldn't remember how the music began.

I shivered. "I don't know if I really want to get on that stage," I told Adam.

Peter walked by just then. He was carrying a tray of hors d'oeuvres.

"Nice dress, Nan," he said. I smiled at him. I wasn't about to tell him I found it at the thrift store.

Then Pamela came over to where we were standing. "Attention, everybody," she called out. "We are ready to begin the evening, so find a comfy place to watch our Willy contest."

The first ones to entertain us were Tom and Juanita. I almost didn't know who they were because they were so dressed up. And they danced the tango like they really knew what they were doing, with all the dips and everything. And they did it on that little stage in the corner. I was amazed.

Next Mrs. Carmichael went up to the stage. She was wearing a red velvet dress with long sleeves and lace at the collar and cuffs. Real old-fashioned. Bobby was with her. He was wearing a hat like they wore in revolutionary times, and was struggling under the weight of a big snare drum.

"Hello, everybody," Mrs. C said. "I learned this poem when I was a child, and I have never forgotten it." She took a deep breath, then began:

Listen my children and you shall hear…

Bobby cupped a hand around his ear and leaned toward the audience.

Of the midnight ride of Paul Revere.

On the eighteenth of April in seventy five;

Bobby traced out '75' in the air, forgetting to make the numbers backward so they would look right to the audience.

Hardly a man is still alive…

"Day-am," Adam whispered, "I hope this is not gonna be one of them real long poems."

Hang a lantern aloft from the belfry arch

In the north church tower as a signal light:

One if by land …

BANG, went Bobby's drum.

And two if by sea…

BANG, BANG

And I on the opposite shore will be…

Bobby shuffled over to the other side of the stage, looking pained as the straps holding his drum up cut into his shoulders.

Ready to ride...

THUMP, THUMP. THUMP, THUMP.

And spread the alarm…

BANG. BANG-BANG-BANG-BANG.

Through every Middlesex village and farm.

Adam whispered again. "What's a Middlesex, Miss Nancy?"

"I think it's just the name of a place, Adam," I whispered back. "But I'm not sure."

Pamela was handing out sheets of paper with *The Midnight Ride of Paul Revere* printed on them, I guess to make it easier for us to follow.

"It's THAT long? Day-am!" Adam said, forgetting to whisper.

It was that long, and before they finally got to the end, Mrs. C's voice was cracking and Bobby looked like he really had been galloping around on a horse all night.

We applauded wildly as they took their bows. We were sure ready for whatever came next.

Pamela announced that there would now be a brief intermission so that people could 'replenish their glasses and partake of edibles.' Peter had taken his ears off and was smoking a cigarette out on the lawn, and Adam had gone home to get his fedora hat, which he said he needed for his act. Pamela's living room was by now crowded with people, and some of them I didn't even know. I would just about rather die than get on that stage, I thought. I went outside and told Peter I was not going to sing the song from Gilligan's Island after all. But thanks so much for teaching me the words, in case I wanted to sing it some other time.

Peter looked at me, frowning. "Stage fright, Nan? I thought you wanted to sing that ridiculous song just because it is ridiculous. What happened to the girl who came to California all gung ho to push the envelope?

"What happened to the friend I spent a whole outrageous day with?"

I didn't answer him.

After a few minutes we took our seats again. Adam was next. He looked like a real movie star with his forties style hat on. He stepped up on the stage, sat down on a wooden stool under the spotlight, and loosened his tie. Then he picked up the microphone and began to sing:

My funny valentine,
Sweet, comic valentine,
You make me smile with my heart...

Mrs. Carmichael, who was sitting in the seat behind me, gasped. I turned around, thinking she was having a heart attack or something. But she was okay.

She leaned toward me and whispered, "That's my favorite song in all the world, Nancy. Frank Sinatra used to sing it better than anybody else. Oh, I do so love this song."

We all loved it, even if it was so old, and when Adam had finished singing, we let him know we loved it.

After Adam took his Frank Sinatra bows, he sat down next to me, and Bobby, who was in back of us next to Mrs. C, asked him if he wanted to trade hats.

"No, sir," Adam said. "No way would I part with my Dobbs Dayton fedora, not even if you was to give me a hundred dollars and a jersey cow."

Pamela was clapping her hands to get our attention. "Who's next?" she wanted to know.

Nobody answered.

"Well, then, I guess I'm next," she said. "I'll be back in a jiffy."

When she got back, a couple of minutes later, she was carrying a brown paper sack and a handful of envelopes. Peter, who had put his ears back on, escorted her to the stage.

"Time for Willies," she announced. But, of course, we had already figured that out. She took two of the little statues out of the bag and held them up.

"Lordy," Adam said. "They look just like Oscars, only their elbows are not stickin' out."

Then she handed one of the envelopes to Peter. "Category: Best Dressed," he said into the microphone. "And the winner is..."

He was opening the envelope. "The winners are…. Tom and Juanita Hendrix."

We all clapped while Tom and Juanita went up to accept their Willy. Tom thanked Wal-Mart for making his outfit possible and his mother for teaching him how to dress himself. And Juanita popped her gum a couple of times to show that fame hadn't changed her one bit.

Bobby and Mrs. Carmichael won for Best Novelty Act and Adam won for Best Overall Presentation. Three acts, three awards. Perfect, I thought.

When I got home, I found an Easter basket with several little chocolate eggs in it on my front porch. Easter eggs. And it wasn't even February yet. I looked to see if the front gate was locked. It was open.

Tomorrow I'm going to the game in S.F. with Roger. But right now I'm going to e-mail Emma and tell her about Pamela's party. And that I'm sorry for telling her to shut up. She's going to be all full of I told you so if she finds out Roger sent me flowers. I think I'll say diddly-squat about that.

I'M SURE YOU ALL KNOW

MEMORANDUM

To: All Tenants
From: Richard Stamp
Date: Friday, February 20th, 2009

I'm sure you all know by now that Betty Carmichael died in her sleep on Thursday. She will be sorely missed. She was a lovely lady and a kindhearted neighbor. Her family has asked that we hold a memorial service here at the Cottages, and the date we have arrived at is one week from tomorrow, Saturday, the 28th. Nancy Lou Walker and Pamela Parker have agreed to coordinate the occasion. Please contact them if you wish to contribute something.
Mrs. Carmichael's family will be coming here from Florida, so let's all pull together to welcome and support them during this difficult time.

> Sincerely,
> Richard Stamp,
> General Manager

I'm still shaking. It was me who found Mrs. Carmichael after she was already dead. I never saw a dead person before, except when I was little at my great-grandfather's funeral where they had the top off of the coffin and we all walked by and looked. But I was holding my Mom's hand then, and anyway I was too short to really see anything.

Well, not this time. This time I saw everything, Mrs. Carmichael lying too still on the couch in her living room with her mouth open and her face real white. Oh! I don't even want to talk about it. I wish I had never gone there that day. I just wanted to say hello, and when I saw that her front door was open, I walked up and called out to her.

"Hi, Mrs. Carmichael." I kept saying her name. "Yoo-hoo Mrs. Carmichael, it's me, Nancy. Are you there, Ma'am?"

But she didn't answer. From the doorway I could see her lying there on her couch, not moving at all, and I knew something was wrong. My heart started to pound. I didn't know what to do. I tried calling Richard, but it was his day off and he wasn't answering his phone. Then I thought of Adam. I ran over to his apartment and knocked as loud as I could on the door.

"Day-am! What is the matter with y'all, bangin' on my door like some wild woman?"

"We have to call 911, Adam, because Mrs. Carmichael is not moving. I think she is, she is, deceased."

"Deceased? Dead? Miss Nancy, she's probably taking a nap, is all."

Adam went back to Mrs. C's apartment with me. He shooed away a couple of flies that were buzzing around her head, and tried to wake her up, while I stayed on the front porch, wishing it was all happening in a dream.

We called 911 and waited for the fire department to get there. Then we told Mr. D what had happened, and he notified the other appropriate people and officials.

Afterwards, Adam asked me if I wanted to go downtown with him, to Spank's. I said no.

"I just want to go home, Adam," I said. "But thanks for asking me."

Now Pamela and me are supposed to plan how we are going to say goodbye to Mrs. Carmichael. I don't even know if she was a Catholic or some other religion, or just preferred to believe in God by herself. I guess her family knows, though, so we can ask them, I suppose.

Then it will mainly be about the food and how many people are coming.

I'm counting on Pamela to know how to do this, because I don't have a clue when it comes to putting on a memorial service. I do think it would be nice to have it down by the river, if it's not too cold, and if it's not raining. And maybe we could have music. She would like that, I think.

GOODBYE, MRS. CARMICHAEL

Today is the day we are saying goodbye to Mrs. C.
Her family is here, staying down the street at the Bridge
House, which is kind of pricey. Mr. D made
arrangements for them to stay there, and it won't cost
them anything because Mr. D is picking up the tab. I can
hardly believe it. But of course everybody loved Mrs. C.

Pamela has thought of just about everything, so I
think we are ready. We are going to have the services or
ceremony or whatever you want to call it by the river,
and Richard and Jimmy have been busy all week cutting
grass and weeds and picking up things and making sure
we can be shipshape and respectful to our friend who
died.

Mrs. C's family says she used to be Catholic but
hasn't attended church for a long time. They think that
we should have a Catholic priest, though, and somebody
from the Quakers, since she so much admired their
peaceful ways.

Adam is doing the flowers, and Juanita is fixing a
lot of food for everybody. Richard is making sure we

have enough drinks. Pamela wanted to have bagpipes, but I talked her out of it. Mrs. C told me once she hated bagpipes. They reminded her of a bunch of squawking chickens, she said. So we are just going to have a boom box.

Peter wants to be in charge of the microphone after the priest says mass. We are hoping people will talk about Mrs. C and what a nice person she was.

Well, it's almost dark now, and people are starting to go home. They did talk about Mrs. C, and what they said put smiles, not tears, on our faces. So many people were there, and so many of them wanted a turn at the microphone. Even her youngest grandson, Zachary, went up there and recited his ABC's. Richard talked about how Mrs. C always made oatmeal-raisin cookies for him on his birthday, real crispy just the way he liked them. And about how she never had an unkind word to say about anybody. And then he talked about how he would miss talking to her on the phone.

"She called me just about every day," he said, "and sometimes… well, I was busy with other things. I just wish…"

But he didn't go on. The words wouldn't come.

Of course, all of us who live at the Cottages were there, well, almost all of us. Bobby and his mother didn't show up.

Most everyone stayed a long time. It was as if Mrs. C was still with us, somehow, and we just couldn't quite say goodbye. When it was finally too dark to see much of anything Adam helped me carry the folding chairs I had brought down back to my apartment. It was one of those times when you just feel like talking to somebody, so I asked Adam if he would like a cup of coffee. "Yes, Ma'am", he said. "I reckon a cup of coffee would taste pretty good right now."

We sat out on my front porch and sipped our coffee. It was a clear night and warm for that time of year. Some of our neighbors were still coming up from the river, on their way back to their apartments.

Then we heard Mrs. C's front door slam. Richard never could get it to fit right, I thought.

"That would be some of her kinfolk, I reckon," Adam said. And after a minute, "Or maybe her critters are back."

We both laughed.

The door slammed a couple of times more.
"Somebody's sure busy over there," Adam said.

And then it began. First the slow, thunderous beat
of the bass drum, then the marching band sound of the
snare drum. A crash of cymbals. Then Frank Sinatra was
singing, '*My funny valentine, my sweet, comic valentine.*'
When the song was over, we heard the beat of the snare
again, a slow, sad 'taps,' loud at first, then getting fainter.
And fainter. And then silence. It was Bobby's goodbye.

I was crying. And so was Adam.

AT LEAST HE WASN'T A REPUBLICAN

I think I'm depressed, maybe because of Mrs. Carmichael being gone. I sure do miss her and wish she could still be here, especially for Bobby.

I miss Roger, too. I broke up with him after we went to the baseball game in San Francisco. On the way home he kept calling me his little okey-dokey Okie, not even paying attention when I told him to stop. And he wouldn't let me drive, even though he knew he shouldn't drive after drinking so much beer. So when we got home I told him I didn't want to go out with him anymore.

In a way, though, I wish I was still seeing him. Like I said, I miss him, even if he was a jerk sometimes. At least he wasn't a Republican, and we did have some good times together. Besides, it's nice to have somebody to take you out, in case you want to go bowling or to the movies, and somebody to cuddle up with when you're watching TV. Maybe what I am is lonesome, not depressed. Or maybe they're both the same thing.

And I feel bad about Blue Louie. It turns out he was the one who was leaving stuff around on people's porches, like the chewing gum and the Easter eggs. That was okay, I guess, even if it did give me the creeps. But he kept coming in at night, climbing over the fence, and that wasn't okay. So when Richard found him wandering around one night by the trash bins he had him arrested for trespassing and acting dangerous. Now he's in jail. It's for his own good, Richard says, so he can get the help he needs. But how is he going to get any help when California can't afford it and Blue Louie doesn't have anybody to stick up for him? When he gets out of jail he'll be right back on the street again, asking people for money and acting weird.

Juanita told me the rodeo is happening this weekend, and there's a parade on Saturday morning. I think I'll ask her if she and Tom want to watch the parade with me.

TWO IN A ROW

We have really had a lot going on around here lately. Last weekend, we had two parades, the rodeo parade on Saturday and the Gay Pride parade on Sunday. The rodeo parade had a lot of horses and some fire trucks, and there was even a pretend shootout. I waved at Bobby when he marched by in the Riverville grammar school band, playing his snare drum.

"I wish Mrs. C could be here to see that," I said to Juanita, who was watching the parade with me.

"Me too," she said.

After the parade, we met Tom for lunch at the Three Bars.

"Sorry I missed the parade," he said. "I had things I needed to do. But I wouldn't miss tomorrow's extravaganza for anything. Wow, two parades in a row. Did it ever occur to you, Nancy, that we live in a pretty egalitarian community?"

I wasn't sure what that meant.

"More like schizophrenic," Juanita said.

I did know what that meant. But I was confused.

"Why do you say that?" I asked.

"Well, look," Tom said, "it's not every town that would put on a parade for the rednecks one day and another one for the queers the next."

"But isn't it wonderful," Juanita added.

I nodded. "It is."

On Sunday, it was threatening to rain, and nobody expected a big turnout for the Gay Pride parade. But the turnout was even bigger than on Saturday. The Sisters had a float and some of our County officials were there. As you would expect, there were lots of balloons in all the rainbow colors. Adam was wearing his Alice costume and was riding with the Sisters, though he doesn't actually belong to their club. Peter was walking behind the women on motorcycles. He was carrying his paper doll without enough clothes on. I waved at him as he passed by, and then all of a sudden I wanted to push the envelope.

"Peter!" I yelled. "Wait up!"

I stepped off the curb and caught up with him. "Give me the doll," I said. I held her in front of me and began singing the song from Gilligan's Island as loud as I could. I wished I had a microphone. I even wished there was a spotlight shining down on me. Peter was laughing so hard he could hardly keep walking, let alone sing. But that was okay because I remembered every word. I didn't need any help from him. And I wasn't just walking. I was dancing. Pretty soon some of the spectators were in the street, dancing with me. And then more and more people joined the parade so that in the end, it was all parade and no parade watchers.

After Sunday's parade I went back to my apartment and called Emma to tell her the first part of June works for me, and I can put her plane reservations on my credit card if she wants me to. I also told her about our two parades and asked her if she didn't think it was wonderful to be so egalitarian. She said she had no idea what I was talking about.

The next day, Monday, we had still more entertainment. It was not a planned event, but it drew a big crowd anyway, especially for a weekday.

THE STANDOFF

Peter came over on Monday night and had dinner with me. I made a tri-tip roast with mushroom sauce, which he said tasted just like his mother's. I guess she uses Campbell's soup to make mushroom sauce, too. We turned on the TV at seven o'clock so we could watch Jeopardy. I'm not very good at Jeopardy, but I like to watch it because I always learn something I didn't know before. And Peter, of course, loves all kinds of trivia type games. We were about halfway through the program, in the middle of the double jeopardy part, and Peter was yelling out, "Who wrote *The Little Prince?*" when somebody pounded on the front door.

"I'll get it," Peter said.

He opened the door, and there was Tom.

"What's up?" Peter asked him.

"Turn on the radio, Buddy Boy," Tom said, "the San Francisco talk show station."

So I turned down the TV, and Peter turned on my radio, the one I keep in case we have an earthquake or a flood and the electricity is not working.

"... at the intersection of Elm Avenue and River Street," somebody was saying, "in the little town of Riverville, just a couple of hours north of San Francisco. About one hundred people are gathered here, hoping to catch a glimpse of the fugitive, who is said to be armed and dangerous."

The station broke for a commercial.

"Hot damn," Peter said. "I've lived in this town for almost five years and in all that time we've never had a fugitive, let alone an armed and dangerous one. Let's go downtown and check it out. It's happening right next door to Spank's, for God's sake."

Just then, the reporter came back on.

"It is believed the fugitive has taken a hostage and has retreated to the attic space of the building. It is not known whether he is still carrying the weapon he used to shoot at an innocent bystander, a bow and arrow, I believe."

"A bow and arrow?" Peter and Tom were both asking the same question.

"This is getting more and more interesting," Peter said. "Let's walk down."

So we walked down to where all the commotion

146

was, or at least as close to all the commotion as we could get. There were so many police cars and fire trucks and television and radio people, with all of their equipment, it was impossible to get any closer than about a half a block away. But we could hear some of what was going on.

Somebody was talking into a bullhorn. "Just come out with your hands up," he was saying. "Nobody will hurt you. Your wife is here. She wants to talk to you."

There was a pause, then a woman's voice. "Honey, please come out. They're going to send little robots in that are equipped with tear gas and can climb the stairs."

That sounds scary, I thought. If I was the fugitive I would sure come out.

"I'm going to try to move in a little closer," Peter said. "Want to come, Nan?"

"It's roped off, Peter, they're not going to let you get any closer."

"Watch me," he grinned.

In a couple of minutes we could see Peter standing next to the sheriff's deputy with the bullhorn.

"Wow," Tom said, "That boy knows the moves."

We stood around for a while, and nothing happened. Then Peter came back, laughing.

"They can't get anything to work," he told us. "They sent the little robots in, and it turned out they couldn't climb the stairs because the stairs are not built to code and the risers are not uniform. The robots evidently can't be programmed to go up stairs that aren't built to code. They tried sending a couple of search and rescue dogs in, but the dogs just disappeared inside the house for a few minutes and then came back out wagging their tails. Now they're going to toss in a cell phone, which the poor guy is probably going to think is some kind of bomb."

"How long has the guy been holed up in the attic?" Tom asked.

"Since last night sometime," Peter said. "The deputy told me they got a 911 call around nine o'clock from somebody who said he was shot at with a bow and arrow as he was walking down the street, and that the arrow had barely missed him and was still buried in a telephone pole. They responded immediately, took pictures of the arrow, and have been here trying to coax the arrow shooter out ever since."

148

"But that's nearly twenty-four hours," I said.

"Ridiculous," Tom added. "A blatant misuse of taxpayers' money. What if he's not even in there? Has anybody actually seen him?"

"I don't think so," Peter said. "But his wife seems to think he's there. What do you say we all adjourn to Spank's while the law figures out what to do next."

So we went over to Spank's. It was crowded, and everybody was talking about how we were on the radio and might even make the ten o'clock news on TV.

"I'm curious about something," Tom said, looking at Peter. "How did you manage to get past everybody who was supposed to be guarding the gate, so to speak, so you could rub elbows with the sheriff's people on the front lines?"

Peter pulled a little card out of his wallet. 'Sheriff's Deputy, Paul Henry Jensen,' it said. 'County of Los Angeles.' There was a faded picture.

"My dad," Peter said. "The date's not really readable anymore, but it's from the seventies. Works every time. But I wouldn't want to pull it out in any kind of situation where using false identification might made things worse." He gave me a knowing look. We were

149

both thinking about how we got pulled over by the highway patrol when we were being outrageous for God.

Just then a bunch more people came into Spank's. "The party's over," somebody said. "They finally got around to doing what they should have done in the first place: enter the house and go after the fugitive."

"And guess what," somebody else said. "He wasn't anywhere to be found. He probably never was."

So we went home, and the media people took our places at Spank's. The Sheriff's people and the fire department radioed each other and filed their reports, and that was the end of the standoff.

I suppose they'll catch the guy who shot the arrow eventually. Or maybe they'll just let it go. I don't really see what they could charge him with. I don't think it's a crime to shoot a telephone pole, and he could always say he didn't know anybody was walking by at the time.

SO, DUDE

When I got home I opened up my laptop and saw that there was an email from Emma.

'So, Dude, how are you?' it began. 'I'm starting to get excited about coming to California. I don't know if I'll even recognize you with your tattoo and your highlights and your California ways, but even if you're a stranger to me I can hardly wait to see you. How am I going to get from the San Francisco airport to Riverville? It doesn't sound like your car has been running all that well.

Emma'

'So Emma', I wrote. 'Why are you calling me Dude? Girls don't call each other Dude. I suppose you think they do in California, but believe me, they don't. And my tattoo doesn't even show with my clothes on. And you are putting highlights in your hair, too, so what's the big deal? I'm going to ask my friend, Adam, if he can take me to the airport. What we should do, I think, is stay over in the city so you can see Chinatown and the cable cars and Fisherman's Wharf before we drive up to Riverville. Adam is gay so we can all just share a room to save money.

Nancy'

I got ready for bed, and was just pulling the covers up over me when I heard my computer make that noise that it makes when somebody sends me an email. I got out of bed and took a look. It was from Emma again.

'We are NOT all going to spend the night in the same room, even if he is gay. Are you crazy????? You're the one who wants to be a California girl, not me. I just want to visit for a few days.

Emma'

THE RADIO SHOW

We have our own radio station in Riverville. The station is on the air twenty-four hours a day, so the people who put on the radio shows are always looking for somebody to interview to fill up the time. Last Thursday, Tom was on the show called, 'Listen Here.' Juanita stopped by in the morning and said I should tune in at two o'clock to hear Tom talk about his great-great-grandfather, who was a Pomo Indian and was just a little boy when the Indians were forced to leave their villages and start living on reservations.

"The radio show hostess is one of Pamela Parker's friends, and she usually has a pretty good program," Juanita said. "I hope Tom doesn't mess with her too much."

When I tuned in, a couple of minutes after two, there was music playing in the background that sounded like ocean waves crashing on the beach, and the radio show hostess was saying, "Listen here, all you folks who need a break from your tweets and your message machines and all those credit card offers. Because today we are going to talk about simpler times and how we might revisit those times in the future. I have some wonderful guests today. Let's start with you, Tom. Tell the people who you are and why you are here."

"Well, this is Tom Hendrix, and I'm not at all sure why I am here," Tom said, "Can I call my wife? She'll know."

"Well, no, Tom, you can't call your wife. On this show people are supposed to call us, not the other way around." She gave a little laugh so Tom would know she understood he was just kidding.

Then a woman's voice came on. "Well, I certainly do know why I am here," she said confidently. "My name is Sharon, and I am the president of Riverville Women for Sustainability. I am here to talk about the beauty of sustainability, the pure gorgeousness of doing things in a sustainable, renewable, earth-friendly way, instead of continuing to plunder the planet, as every male-dominated generation before us has done."

"Really," Tom said.

"And I represent 'Just Green,' another woman's voice chimed in. Green technology's time has come. We can no longer ignore the fact that if our biological

154

systems are to endure and remain productive, we will have to bring together our economic, social and biological spheres."

"Well, I'm all for long lasting biological systems," Tom said. "I hope I'll be around for at least another thirty years. But it seems to me the Indians knew all about this stuff a long time ago. The Pomos, for example, who lived in this area for thousands of years, had very little impact on the environment. They were hunters and gatherers, and until large numbers of them were wiped out by the cavalry in 1850, they were leading pretty sustainable lives."

"Tom's great-great-grandfather was a Pomo Indian," the hostess said. "Would you like to tell us about him, Tom?"

"Yes. My great-great-grandfather was only five years old when his family was sent to a reservation."

"Excuse me," still another voice broke in. "My name is Amber and I would like to say that I used to put everything in the garbage, I mean everything, but I now re-cycle to the hilt. You might say I'm a recovering dumpaholic." She giggled.

"And you do your re-cycling one day at a time, I

suppose," Tom said.

"Well, how else would I do it?" she asked, not getting the joke.

There was a station break, and then still another voice, a man's this time.

"Did you know there is an enormous area in the middle of the ocean that is nothing but solid plastic?" he asked. "I am forming a committee here in Riverville to see what can be done about that. We are having a fund-raiser next weekend. Tickets are available at the five and dime and also at The Bird's Nest."

Then the woman named Sharon was talking about sustainability again. I listened for a little while, hoping to hear more about Tom's great-great-grandfather, but Tom didn't seem to have anything more to say, or if he did, nobody was giving him a chance to say it. So I switched off the radio and e-mailed Emma:

'Hi Emma,

There is so much I want to show you. I can hardly wait for you to get here. Do you want me to make an appointment for you to get a tattoo?

The bartender at Spank's says he has invented a new drink just for you, and Peter says he will take you for a ride in the Impala if you will wear a princess crown and a beauty pageant banner.

Nancy'

RICHARD'S DAY IN COURT

MEMORANDUM

To: Apartments C thru E, G, K, and anybody else who was living here when Evonna Courtland occupied apartment B last year.
From: Richard Stamp
Date: May 26th, 2009
RE: Strategy Meeting

     We regret to say that Evonna Courtland has filed a suit in small claims court about the way she says she was treated before leaving the Cottages in August of last year. The case is scheduled for next Monday at the County Center in Hennington. I know this is short notice, I didn't find out myself until yesterday exactly when we were scheduled. I would like to meet with the above referred to people to see if any of you can go on Monday and/or have anything to say about Miss Courtland's behavior previous to being evicted.

     Yours truly,
     Richard

So I guess Richard finally ran out of postponements. We never got around to holding a meeting. But Adam, Peter, Juanita and me all showed up in the parking lot at 8:30 a.m. on Monday morning. Tom had to work.

Adam had his hair neatly tied back in a ponytail, and Mr. D was dressed in a brown suit and brown suede shoes. He was sporting a tie, and had a briefcase tucked under his arm. I must say he looked real official. The rest of us just looked like our regular selves.

Nobody had a clue what was going to happen or what we were supposed to do about it. Mr. D said we should elect somebody to be our spokesperson, just in case the Judge wanted to hear from us, so we elected Peter unanimously, and he said he would be honored. But wouldn't you know, when we got to the courthouse, security wouldn't let him in because people in flip-flops are not allowed to be in the Judge's presence. Who ever heard of such a dumb rule? Juanita was wearing sandals, and that was okay with security. If women's bare toes are appropriate in court, then men's should be, too, is what I think.

So here we were, everybody except Peter, inside the courthouse, and I for one still didn't know what Evonna was claiming Richard did to her that caused her so much pain and suffering. A lawful looking woman told us to be seated in the courtroom and then called out our names to see if we were really there. Then she told us to go back out in the lobby and try one more time to patch things up so we wouldn't waste the Judge's time. Since just the main, principal parties were needed for this stage of the proceedings, I decided to go outside and tell Peter what was happening.

"So they're trying to mediate," Peter said. "That ought to be interesting. Maybe security will let me in if I promise to stay in the lobby."

Peter took off one of his flip-flops and showed the security guard the label on the bottom. "Best thongs available in any store," he said. "Cost me a bundle."

The guard let him in.

We could see that Richard and Mr. D and Evonna and another woman were standing together a few feet away from us. But we couldn't hear what they were saying.

"I have to pee," Peter announced, and headed for the men's room, which was just past where Richard and the rest of them were standing. He was back in a couple of minutes.

161

"Fat chance this is going to work," he said. "She just called him a bastard."

I was shocked. "The mediator woman called Richard a bastard?"

"No, silly girl, Evonna called him that."

I was going to ask Juanita what she thought about it, but when I turned to ask her I saw that she was sitting at the security guard's table and was chatting with him. He was showing her pictures, I guess of his grandchildren, and she was saying, "Oh, how cute is that! You must be so proud."

A line began to form on the other side of the table.

"Yoo-hoo, Mr. Guard," somebody said. "I'm ready to be searched." But the guard wasn't paying attention. So people just started walking right past him. It didn't seem to matter anymore what shoes they were wearing or what they had in their purses. Of course, it was just small claims court, not the Pentagon, but still...

The Bailiff announced that the Judge was now ready to hear our cases, and we went back into the courtroom. I sat down next to Adam, and then we all stood up again while the Judge came in. She was younger than I'd figured she would be and was smiling.

She looked like a real nice person.

Our case was called right away. Mr. D and Richard stood behind a table, facing the Judge, and Evonna stood behind another table, all by herself, a few feet away. She wasn't wearing much makeup, just some pale pink lipstick, and she looked tired. I wondered where she was living now and whether anyone had come with her to the courthouse.

Mr. D. emptied out his briefcase and stared seriously at his official papers. Richard didn't have anything to stare at. He just stood there and tried to make his muscles not twitch. He's nervous, I thought. He doesn't like having to defend himself in public against a crazy woman.

Evonna was looking at some kind of little book, it looked to me like a notebook.

"Holy Moses," Adam whispered. "She even kept a journal."

"Time to begin," smiled the Judge. Then she asked Evonna, the Plaintiff, to state her case. So she did. In her little Jackie O voice she explained how she moved here from the state of Washington in February of 2008 and just loved Riverville, until she moved in to the Cottages, where one Richard Stamp was employed as General Manager. At first everything was okay, she said, but after she refused the General Manager's 'very insistent and unwelcome advances' sometime in June, her life was all down hill. She began to have stomach cramps and painful headaches and trouble sleeping, all because of the General Manager. She turned and glared at Richard, just to make sure we all knew who she was talking about.

Adam and me looked at each other, amazed.

"Miss Courtland, can you give me a specific example of the General Manager's inappropriate demeanor toward you?"

Evonna turned the pages of her little book.

"Well, Your Honor, for instance, on July 5th of 2008 he told me I could no longer park my car in my assigned parking space or anywhere else inside the gate at the Cottages, even though my rent was all paid up."

Adam nudged me. "I reckon we know why that was," he whispered.

"I complained to the owner," Evonna went on, and he let me park in one of the places next to his house temporarily. But then he told me, the General Manager, not the owner, I couldn't keep my car there either."

"Just a minute, Miss Courtland," interrupted the Judge. "Would you care to comment on any of these allegations, Mr. Stamp?"

Richard glanced at Mr. D, who was still studying his official papers. Then he cleared his throat and began to talk.

"Well, Sir, first of all..."

"Your Honor," corrected the Judge.

"Yes. Well, Miss Courtland ran over my belongings with her car on July Fourth, and I was afraid she might do it again. That's why I didn't want her to park anywhere inside the gate beginning July 5th."

"How was she able to run over your belongings with her car?" asked the Judge. "Were your belongings in the street?"

"Yes, Sir, Your Honor, I mean. She carried them out of my apartment and put them in the street."

"Was she staying at your apartment with you?"

"No."

"Did she have a key to your apartment?"

"No," Richard said, but he didn't sound so sure.

"Yes I did! Yes I did!" Evonna said.

"Please don't interrupt, Miss Courtland," the Judge said.

Richard went on. He was blushing. "And the reason I asked her to move her car out of the owner's parking space was because it was leaking oil. I told her to get it fixed, but she just ignored me. Leaking oil is something we don't put up with at the Cottages." He was gripping the edge of the table in front of him so hard his knuckles were white.

"Richard is not liking this, Miss Nancy," Adam whispered in my ear.

"I think he's embarrassed," I said.

The Judge turned to Evonna. "Miss Courtland, is there something more you would like to add?"

Evonna nodded. "This little book is full of notes I jotted down about Mr. Stamp's irrational and bizarre behavior, behavior which finally caused me to take up residence elsewhere." She looked up at the Judge and forced a smile. "But I know you are a busy person, Your Honor, and have other cases to hear today, so I shall describe to you just one incident, a most shocking incident that clearly shows Richard Stamp's disregard of commonly accepted safety standards." She was turning the pages of her little book again, and I noticed her hands were shaking.

"Please just get to the point, Miss Courtland," the Judge said.

"Well, the point is, Your Honor, the Cottages are surrounded by wild raccoons, everybody knows that." She looked over in our direction, like she was expecting us to back her up.

"They often watch people through the windows and will grab any opportunity to come into an apartment and attack a person, with the goal of dragging that person back to their dens."

"Back to their dens?" the Judge asked, her eyebrows raised.

"Oh yes, Your Honor. One evening a particularly large male raccoon came out of my living room wall and..."

Somebody giggled.

The Judge's eyebrows shot up again. "Miss Courtland," she asked, "what does this have to do with the Defendant, Mr. Stamp?"

"I'm getting to that, Your Honor. Mr. Stamp will deny it, I'm sure, but the raccoon was in my wall because he put it there after I refused to marry him."

She glared at Richard again. "That's the kind of man he is, Your Honor, and…"

"Miss Courtland, did you consult a doctor about your various ailments, and do you have the medical records to show that you did, while you were a tenant at Smoke Hill Cottages?"

There was no answer.

"Do you have any witnesses who can testify that you were attacked by raccoons and/or other wild animals while you lived at the Cottages?"

No answer.

"Well then, I believe we are wasting everybody's time. Let me see if I understand you correctly. You are alleging that the Defendant in this case, Richard Stamp, caused you pain and suffering for which you should be compensated. But you have no evidence to support your claim. Is that correct?"

"Yes, but I would just like to say…."

People had started whispering and moving around in their seats, and the Judge slammed her gavel down to get our full attention back.

"Miss Courtland, I think we have all heard quite enough. I do not see any kind of legal case here. I hereby rule in favor of the Defendant. Case dismissed."

So Richard won. And Mr. D got to keep the money Evonna wanted for her pain and suffering. Richard thanked us for spending our time and bought us all lunch. It felt real good knowing we did the right thing, by showing up for our General Manager in his time of need.

But I still don't get it. Why did Evonna think anybody would believe her? That stuff about Richard putting raccoons in the wall was just ridiculous. And she made it sound like she was never the least bit interested in Richard, when actually she was hoping he would ask her to marry him.

They were being pretty cozy with each other that time I saw them on the pool deck right before the Fourth of July, so maybe he did give her a key to his apartment. But so what? It's not a crime to give a person a key to your apartment.

I wonder what really happened to make Evonna want to run over Richard's stuff and then try to make him look bad in court. Evonna can't tell us because she doesn't know what's real and what's just in her head, and Richard isn't talking. So I guess we'll never know. What I think, though, is that Evonna's imagination got carried away, pure and simple. Richard does have awesome blue eyes.

I do feel sorry for Evonna, though. I wonder what it's like to be crazy. It must feel real scary and real lonesome when nobody is on your side because you are acting so weird.

It's going to be the Fourth of July again pretty soon. We just got a memo about it. Richard keeps saying he wants to quit his job and go some place that's far away from Riverville.

What will everybody do then? Without Richard this place is just going to fall apart. There'll be fish in the swimming pool again, and homeless people hanging around, waiting to escort somebody home from Spank's or that new bar that just opened up the street. I don't want to be here then.

EMMA COMES TO TOWN

June 15, 2009

I just got back from visiting Nancy in California. It's just Nancy now, not Nancy Lou. We rode on the cable cars and saw the sights in San Francisco. That was fun. And we stayed overnight at the Fairmont Hotel, which is the fanciest place I've ever been to. Nancy's friend, Adam, stayed at the Fairmont with us, but of course he had his own room.

I don't know what I was expecting Riverville to be like. It's smaller than I thought it would be, that's for sure. There's no Wal-Mart and no MacDonald's, but there's an old-fashioned five and dime store with saltwater taffy and licorice and lots of toys for little kids. That's where I found t-shirts for everybody back home.

I asked Nancy if she ever saw Roger, and she said no. Then I told her that Henry is engaged to marry Alice Wood.

"Henry who?" she asked.

"Henry Thomas Hampton the third," I told her.

"Oh, him," she said.

"Well, Nancy, you did go out with him for two whole years. I really don't know why you're acting like you can't even remember who he is."

I also asked her if a lot of boys were getting married to each other in California. She told me they can't marry each other anymore. Because the people voted to change the law back to the way it was before.

"But it will change again," she said. "Someday the rest of California will be as egalitarian as Riverville."

Whatever that's supposed to mean, I thought.

We were sitting at the bar at Spank's one night when Nancy told me she was going to pack up and leave Riverville in a few weeks.

"Mom and Dad are loaning me some money so I can turn in my car for a newer one," she said. "Then I am going to travel all over the United States, or at least as far as I can get before I run out of money for gas. There must be someplace where most of the cute guys aren't gay."

"But Nancy," I said. "I don't understand. I thought you wanted to be a California girl."

She laughed. "Don't be silly, Emma. Being a California girl doesn't have anything to do with where you actually live. I thought you knew that."

And then she asked me, "Are you really going to get a tattoo? Where are you going to put it?"

I grinned. "Wouldn't you like to know."

*

Acknowledgments

Thanks to family and friends for their encouragement.

Thanks to Cheryl Strawn for her enthusiasm early on, without which I might not have taken the next step.

Thanks to Jake Hamlin for being so upbeat about the book, and especially for his help with the story line and for his willingness to spend so much time with me zeroing in on what worked and what didn't.

Thanks to the *Sisters of Perpetual Indulgence* for permission to refer to them in this book.

Thanks to Sandra Maresca for her wonderful graphics. You might want to visit her website at www.croneclown.com.

And of course, thanks to my editor, Birgit Nielsen, who held my hand through all of the steps to publication, and whose high standards of professionalism insisted I stay with this project until we both could say it was truly complete. I shall be forever in her debt.

And finally, thank you, Don Bach, former General Manager at Fire Mountain Lodge. I know. It didn't really happen that way. But it could have. I dedicate this book to you.

GWH

www.ingramcontent.com/pod-product-compliance
Lightning Source LLC
Chambersburg PA
CBHW072140170626
46813CB00004BA/1623